The Bangkok Fiasco and other Stories

The Bangkok Fiasco and other Stories

Subroto Bandopadhyay

Vitasta

At the Lotus Feet of
Ma Kali

This book is dedicated to my late parents
I wish they were here to read it and enjoy.
And also, to all the relatives and friends
For encouraging and nurturing this dreamy boy!

Published by
Renu Kaul Verma
Vitasta Publishing Pvt Ltd
2/15, Ansari Road, Daryaganj
New Delhi - 110 002
info@vitastapublishing.com

ISBN: 978-81-948200-0-0

First Edition 2021
MRP ₹ 350

Edited by Veena Batra
Typeset & Cover Design by Somesh Kumar Mishra
Printed by Vikas Computer and Printers, New Delhi

Contents

Preface

The Bangkok Fiasco and Other Stories is a compilation of nine short stories. It was quite difficult to find an appropriate name for such a collection. So, I chose the catchiest story title.

I am a retired Group Captain of the Indian Air Force, the most elite force of our beloved motherland. But, as they say, 'the Rank never retires, it's you who retire'. So, I proudly call myself a Gp Capt and a veteran, and shall continue to do so till my last breath. Being an active and well-qualified flying branch officer (Navigator, to be precise), I had plenty of opportunities to go abroad. I was the first privileged Indian to navigate an IL-76 aircraft of IAF successfully around the world in 2003, though it was with multi-stops. I also had the unique distinction of navigating the same IL-76 aircraft from the Eielson Air Base of USAF in Alaska, over the True North Pole and back. This particular flight finds a mention in the Limca Book of Records. During such visits to various countries, I did come across a lot of Indians settled abroad. And believe me, Indians settled abroad are 'more Indian' than we can actually imagine. I have met an elderly Sardarji (Sorry I don't recollect the gentleman's name) who runs a dhaba, catering mostly for the Indian students studying in the University in Fairbanks, Alaska. I have also witnessed Durga puja in Moscow where not only Bengalis but all Indians, irrespective of caste, creed and religion dutifully participate to make it a success. Honestly speaking, Indian diaspora is an absolutely fantastic lot.

Human life is an assortment of short stories. Some stories are romantic, some tragic, some sceptic, a few opportunistic. There are stories of hope, of pain, of sudden windfall, of despair, of values, of violence and of sacrifices. Here are a few of these, just for you! Some of the stories written in this book are inspired by real life incidents that actually happened around me. But most other stories are figments of my imagination.

Each one of us has encountered many odd/ awkward/ funny or desperate situations or moments during the course of our lives, some of which may be worth sharing with others. If you would like to do so, please share your experiences with me. It may encourage me to pen a sequel to this book in due course of time. I thank Ankita, my elder daughter, for being a real critique and my invaluable proofreader. I also thank Akshit, my son-in-law, for all the e-support. Many thanks to Shillpi, my younger daughter, for all the moral support and timely encouragement and to dear Rita, my ailing, otherwise impatient wife, for being so patient with me all this while!

And of course, my sincere thanks to Renu, Veena and the entire team of Vitasta Publications for making my dream come true!

Happy Landings! Oops! Happy Reading!

Bydgoszcz Diary

Dr Anand Kumar Dey has recently returned from Poland. For him, Poland was, and is, 'a nothing to write home about' country in Europe. As everyone knows and appreciates, probably barring Germany and a few Islamic countries, all other countries are generally addrcssed as Motherland by their respective countrymen. So, She, I mean Poland, does not hold a significant place in the world's political, financial, technological or sports arena today. But her geographical location within Europe is strategically very important, rather was very important during Second World War. Lying sandwiched between Germany and Russia (then USSR), the country was invaded twice between 1939 and 1945. At the beginning of the war, in order to conquer USSR, the Germans first entered Poland from the West, killed scores of able-bodied men, put thousands of Jews in gas chambers, maimed most children and raped all the women they came across while walking through the country's aesthetic landscape. At the end of the war, the Russians, chasing the 'by now beleaguered' Germans, invaded Poland from the East and repeated the same barbaric acts on her peace-loving citizens for no fault of theirs! In last couple of decades, the country may have come out of the physical hurt and psychological trauma she was subjected to, but has not forgiven the rogue neighbours completely.

Anand Dey, anglicised 'Andy' by himself and some of his close friends, had finished his Class 12 Board exams from an English medium school in Bhagalpur, Bihar, in the science stream. Though 100 per cent rice and fish eating Bengalis, his family has been living in this small town of Bihar for generations. In fact, his grandfather was a zamindar here. Andy is quite fair and a little on the heavier side, thanks to lots of baby fat accumulated all around his 206 bones over the years, kind courtesy of desi ghee and butter. Hence, his mostly Bihari schoolmates (where English is generally taught in Hindi medium) and neighbour's children did not waste much time to nickname him 'Anday' meaning eggs, which he loathes till date from the bottom of his heart.

Andy alias Anday didn't come out of school with so-called flying colours exactly, but did reasonably well for himself. Like most other students of his group and their restless parents, search for a good medical college began in earnest. But India genuinely has a huge demand supply gap in this area, where total MBBS seats are in thousands but the aspirants are in lacs, progressively soaring towards crore! Competition is so severe that only the students scoring more than 90 per cent or with good amount of push-and-pull are generally entertained, even in private colleges.

So, after a while it became clear that with 87 per cent and without any other backing, he did not stand a chance to secure an MBBS seat in any reasonably good college in India. So, his parents frantically started looking for options outside. None of the Dey family members had ever been abroad as such, probably except to neighbouring Nepal. But as an erstwhile zamindar family, they had enough financial resources to fund his studies abroad. And everyone wanted him to fulfil his illiterate late Grandma's last wish, 'to see him as a doctor'.

Out of the four countries finally shortlisted, China was almost immediately ruled out by his 49-year-old, issueless, divorced at 31, staying with them ever since, cotton sari-clad, vociferous, pure vegetarian, (except fish, obviously!)'Pishima' (paternal aunt) who didn't want to see him becoming a 'Frog-Eater'! No more arguments, so, first case—closed.

His mother refused to send him to a medical college in Nepal. "How can I face my relatives and neighbours? Nepal is not a 'Foreign Country' for us Indians! It's just a few hours road journey from here. After deciding to spend so much money for his foreign-education, I won't be able to stand the ridicule of those stupid ladies in kitty parties! Nepal, no way." Second option rejected too, rather unceremoniously!

Similarly, the next option of sending him to the Russian Medical College in Moscow was turned down by his father. He opined that he was very apprehensive about the extreme cold weather prevailing there during most part of the year. But the actual fact was, he was mortally scared of the KGB. He did not want his only son to land up in some 'Labour Concentration Camp' in God-forsaken Siberia! You never knew these KGB guys!

Now everyone looked intently at the only option left—Collegium Medicum in Bydgoszcz, Poland. Shri Google was not born then. And if at all born in the USA, did not exist in India those days (1990s) to enlighten the instant knowledge seekers. So, all the family members ran around in circles looking for some clippings, articles, anything about this rather funny sounding place. After a number of intense in-house healthy discussions, some not-so-healthy debates and a few near-violent arguments, Poland received the much-anticipated Thumbs Up by all! Well, as if the family actually had some other choice! Huh...

After a good amount of preparations and fanfare, Anand was given a decent send-off from Bhagalpur by his family and friends, six years ago. They were fairly rich by Bhagalpur standards but not so very affluent at the same time. So, it was unanimously decided that, come what may, he would return home only after becoming a doctor. No unnecessary, highly avoidable recurring expenditure on return tickets every year. Period!

Going out of India for the first time to a country so far away, that too for such a long time, wasn't easy for 18-year-old Anand. But with his in-born smartness, intelligence and a little bit of luck, he sailed through fairly smoothly. Now, Dr Anand Dey, 24-year-old, first ever doctor of the renowned zamindar family, is back in Bhagalpur, looking mature and very doctorly!

"Oh my God! You have become so bloody fair! Looks like an angrez saheb, doesn't he?"

"Don't tell me you have come back alone? Where is your memsaab?"

"Show us what gifts you have got for each one of us! Otherwise we won't let you enter the house at all!"

Such exhaustive cross-questioning by the extremely happy family members and home-coming celebrations went on for a week. Then he decided to start his own clinic in a medium-sized room with an attached toilet, on the outer flank of his big ancestral house.

Like majority of highly educated Indians who keep a small library at home, he too decided to literally showcase all his 'carefully brought back' valuable books on Medicine in his clinic. Being very touchy about this, he took on the task himself and started stacking the books on the wall-mounted glass shelves. While meticulously trying to do so, a miniature notebook popped out and fell from between two fat books. Anand bent down to pick it up, looked at it and smiled. Sweet old memories came back to him instantly. Anuradha Srivastava, his classmate till class 12, had given him this parting gift—a flowery baby-pink small note book, bound hard, along with a soft kiss! The first and only kiss from a young and beautiful girl obviously, received by him in India till date! So, he had made it a point to carry this precious gift all the way to Poland for two reasons; firstly, as a soulful sole remembrance from Annu and secondly, to use it as a diary. He inscribed an apt name on its cover, 'Bydgoszcz Diary'.

He decided to jot down all possible big or small, day to day happenings from the time his maiden journey towards Poland began. But slowly gave up maintaining the diary regularly because of sheer pressure of studies. In fact, he almost forgot about its very existence, especially after Anuradha's marriage. Well, that happened sometime during the third year. She had called him up just before her wedding to Ram Parvesh Mahto, a mutually known, tenth pass, successful local businessman. She had pleaded with him desperately to do something; either get the wedding itself called off or postponed indefinitely. But being so far away from home, still a student, professionally unsettled and from a rather conservative family, he did not have the guts to speak to his parents about his own wedding! That too by making an expensive ISD call! He felt absolutely helpless and just let it go. He did love Annu but the prevailing circumstances did not allow him to act heroic.

Anyway, she was happily married now, expecting her first baby; he had found out secretly. And after so many one-night-stands abroad in last six years, he didn't really miss her. Or did he ...? He was not sure.

He sat down on a plastic chair and started sifting through the pages leisurely reading his own Bydgoszcz Diary: -

03 Sept, Somewhere in the sky between Moscow and Warsaw

The aeroplane has finally taken off. Looking at her huge size I was wondering how does it go up in the air? But now it's up in the sky for last one hour and I'm loving it! The aeroplane which brought me from Delhi to Moscow was much smaller in size. Both are Aeroflot planes. But this one is scheduled to proceed to London after dropping some of us at Warsaw. Obviously, it is carrying plenty of passengers. I had slept a lot in that six-hour long flight between Delhi and Moscow. So, I'm wide awake now.

Feeling lucky to get a window seat I am loving watching the aeroplane tearing through the white clouds. For the first time ever, I've seen clouds so closely! They look like a massive collection of freshly sorted cotton, at least thousand times bigger than the piles I've seen lying outside the desi quilt making shops on the streets of Bhagalpur! So fascinating! Wow!

After politely enquiring about my meal preferences, the six-foot-tall 'KGB Agent looking' airhostess served me non-veg dinner. It was quite a while since my last meal so, I was extremely hungry. Therefore, without wasting any time, I quickly savoured what seemed like mutton and rice. The meat pieces were very soft and juicy and the meal was hot! After I burped with satisfaction I heard a female voice from behind, distinctively Indian, calling the airhostess. "Can you please give me veg food? I am a Hindu so I don't eat beef."

Beef? Oh my God! How can it be? I had a non-veg meal in the last Aeroflot flight too but the Indian airhostess on board had served me chicken!

"Sorry, we serve only beef for non-vegetarians in this flight. I'll get you veg food soon," the airhostess replied in a matter-of-fact way.

But for me, the damage has already been done. Not even 24 hours have passed since I've left the Indian soil and I have eaten one full plate of beef! I've committed an outrageous act! I must be the only scoundrel in my entire clan of all past and maybe future generations to have had beef. This is in no way pardonable. I can't tell this to anyone, not even to Annu! This has to remain a secret with me unto death.

5th Sept, Bydgoszcz

I've reached my destination at last. After spending one night in the beautiful capital city of Warsaw, I took a train from there last evening and arrived at Bydgoszcz railway station this morning. Just outside the small but neat and clean railway station, I saw a '25 something' young woman selling cosmetic items spread across a small folding table. She looked towards me, gave a brief but sweet smile and signalled. I have never, ever been signalled by any girl or woman that way before. Yes, back home, I had signalled quite a few of them in last two years. Some ignored me and a few showed the terrifying backside of their sandals. Only one had come close, very very close, to slap me hard! Never mind, I have forgiven that girl! Bygones are bygones, you see! It's part of life, part of growing up! Anyway, bemused, I slowly went to her lugging my heavy baggage. "You Indie! You want this?" She asked waving two thin, longish packets at me. Oh Ma! She is selling agarbattis made in Mysore! Can you believe it!

I later found out that the city had a sizeable number of Indians, mostly students. Some of them got these kinds of essential items while coming back from India after every mid-term break and sold them to her at a marginal profit. The others sincerely bought from this woman. Well, how would the Indian students pass the exams otherwise without doing regular puja and taking the blessings of at least one of the crores of Gods and Goddesses as a return gift! No way! Not even Anand Kumar Dey!

6th Sept, Hostel

I was reading the history of Poland. I realised every country and every city here in Europe has a peculiar story to tell. Though the local script is English they don't pay much attention towards using vowels. Take Bydgoszcz for instance, it's pronounced as Bidgosh. History says the actual name probably was 'Be the guest' as the residents then were supposed to be very hospitable. Over a period of time it has become such a tongue-twister! Secondly, this small but beautiful city is located on the banks of an equally small but fairly clean river 'Brda'. Sorry, I don't really know how to pronounce it; Brada, Brida or Broda?

Well, the natives of Poland are known as Polish and are also fondly called 'Poles'; I wonder what the people of Holland are called? 'Holish' or 'Holes'? Ha…ha…ha….

7th Sept

I never had more than hundred rupees in my pocket in school days. But today, in this European country I've suddenly become very rich! Baba had given me forty-six thousand rupees specifically for forex. This I exchanged at Delhi before leaving and managed to get one thousand US Dollars. Today, I got the entire amount exchanged to local currency and got 69,000 Zlotys per Dollar which translates to One Rupee = 1500 Zlotys. That makes it, oh my God! 46,000 multiplied by 1,500!! That makes it 69,000,000 Zlotys, I mean cool 6 Crores 90 Lac Zlotys in my pocket! Crorepati of another type! Hey Bhagwan, Jai Ma Kali!

Friday, the 13th

Had a very memorable experience today. After completion of all arrival formalities, the much awaited MBBS course of mine finally started a few days back. Today being the beginning of the weekend and with no pending homework, I had nothing to do in the evening. So, I decided to venture out to the local market for some quality time pass. It was quite delightful to see either young girls or middle-aged women manning or should

I say 'womanning' majority of the stores. All of them are so fair and beautiful! Though language is a big problem here but their smiles say it all. So disarming, welcoming and undoubtedly friendly!

Leisurely walking amongst a lot of Poles I approached the eastern end of the small market. The extreme corner shop somehow caught my attention. It was a women's undergarment shop owned by a very good-looking woman in her late twenties I presumed. What actually had caught my greedy eyes was an equally beautiful teenage girl standing in front of the shop. She was trying to size up a new bra over her T-shirt by actually putting it on! Well, I had never seen such a scene before! One could never imagine seeing this in a market in India! Indian girls hesitantly walk into a shop, very sheepishly ask for a particular brand and size, quickly pay for it, get it wrapped and leave discreetly, especially in Bhagalpur. So, it was a real eye popper for a Bhagalpurian like me. Looking at my surprised face, the teenager dished out a cute, warm smile. One week's stay and the general friendliness shown by the womenfolk here have made me rather smart and bold. Is that because of my good looks or the tanned skin? I really don't know! So, this 'Bold Bong-Bihari' gathered courage and went near the 'Beautiful Pole' to have a closer look. Observing my advance, the shopkeeper whispered something into her prospective client's ears. By now I was just a few steps away from the teenager. The cutie looked at me again, gave a naughty smile and suddenly removed her T-shirt in front of the entire crowd! Her bare and fair upper torso just had a small pink bra covering the essentials! She now started trying out the new bra over her old one! I was embarrassed, bewildered and mesmerised by it all. Seeing my mixed expressions, both the girls in the shop and others gathered around me by now suddenly burst out laughing. I realised they had played a prank on me; as per their standards, an innocent one!

Her name is Indira, Indira Cherosky. Surprised by the name, aren't you? Well, there is a story behind it. As part of a University Educational Tour, her mother had visited India in early eighties. There she was absolutely overwhelmed by our culture and Mrs Indira Gandhi, then Prime Minister. Later she named her only daughter Indira. Lo and behold! I had already befriended her. She appeared more than willing to speak to me in her broken English. Maybe she has fallen for my innocence! Or my sheer stupidity? Or my tanned body! Or is it just because I'm an Indian? Anyway, who cares! She is so cute!

Who the hell says Friday the 13th is an unlucky day?

Anand took a break. He closed the diary and poured tea from the flask sent by Pishima through Ramu kaka, their old, pre-historical, faithful Man Friday. Sipping tea, a lot of sweet European memories came back to him and made him smile.

He flipped through the dairy again and settled down to read the particular page which contained his most painful experience abroad…

7th October

Thirteen has proved to be a good number for me so far. Well, at least once! But today, number 7 came out to be a really bad one. Unlucky 7!

I had gone to the coffee joint close by to unwind and to take a break from my boring studies—Bone Structure of Human Body. After placing the order for coffee and a plate of finger chips, I occupied the only table lying vacant, just opposite the cash counter. Sitting idle my greedy pair of eyes started roving and probing around the small room. They were generally scanning for some young and beautiful smiling faces, or something more interesting. They finally stopped at the counter. There was this '30 something' lady, a sexy looking one. She was the cashier there, probably the owner too. I had just paid her for my small order but I did not look at her properly that time. Now I realised that the top two buttons of her white silk blouse were open, exposing her cleavage in a big way! My hungry eyes were delighted. So, I kept on staring at her half-exposed pair of breasts continuously as she continued to do her job of collecting cash and passing the customers' orders to the kitchen quite unmindfully. Whenever she looked up and her eyes met mine, she smiled. That typical friendly Polish smile! Maybe she hadn't realised it. I was enjoying myself thoroughly.

After a while, may be about five odd minutes later, a young man nearly my age walked in. He, too, went to the cashier first, paid and placed his order, and then sat at the next table. Almost immediately he got up from his seat and walked back to the cash counter. I felt a little startled. Standing there he stared back at me and gave a wry smile.

Oh shit! This man had probably seen me looking at her milk-white breasts, leching at her. Damn him!

He then turned towards the woman at the counter, bent down and gently buttoned her blouse! In response, she softly caught and pulled his head down and planted a 'Thank You' motherly kiss on his forehead. No, she was not that old! Maybe it was an elder sister's kiss and nothing more. A good job, a noble deed done, the boy now came back to his chair and sat down quietly, as if nothing had happened.

But believe you me, a lot happened inside me! I felt very small and terribly ashamed of myself!

Am I a man? No respect for elderly ladies! What kind of Indian am I? What would these Poles think about me? I had no answers.

I left the coffee shop straightaway, without waiting for the coffee and my favourite finger chips to arrive. I had already paid for my order, so it didn't really matter. I almost ran back to the hostel. I couldn't face this lady and that young man ever in my life!

Dr Anand closed the diary and gently kept it aside. He started recollecting the entire episode, that shameful incident, over and over again. Analysing it deeply, he understood that the young man who shamed him that day, actually possessed a good moral character! And the ease with which the lady trusted and allowed this man to touch her and button her silk blouse in full public view! Absolutely admirable! She too had a beautiful mind.

Maybe this is what is actually called 'A National Character'. That of mutual trust and admiration which goes a long way, beyond the narrow boundaries of religion, caste, creed, politics, age, gender and sexual orientation; to respect, admire and protect each other, especially from the external threats from creepy aliens like me. Poland is a small, non-descriptive country for most of us but the people have unbelievable moral character.

And we, Indians? We belong to one of the world's oldest civilisations; have a very colourful heritage, and an extremely rich culture. But unfortunately, we are absolutely mannerless. We break traffic rules day in and day out, we men ogle at women of all ages, from a seven-year-old innocent child to seventy-year-old grandma! Each one of us thinks that breaking the queue anywhere is our birthright. We pick up fights at the slightest provocation. We don't return the extra change erroneously given by the poor tea seller, the poorest of all traders! We have no morality, and no national character! What a great contrast!

On a lighter note, the Polish are *Polished* and we Indians are *Unpolished!*

A Loving Wife

"What the Hell are you doing inside the toilet for such a long time?" screamed Janaki.

"What do other people do inside the toilet? Bharatnatyam? Or Kuchipudi dance? I'm just doing the big job, early morning wala. What's wrong with you?" shouted back Janaki Raman with matching vocal power.

Hearing his scream and realising how angry her husband actually was, Janaki backtracked quietly to the bedroom. She now lay on the bed sobbing uncontrollably.

Janaki Raman was indeed very agitated and angry with Janaki, his wife for last thirty-odd years. Of late she had been troubling him a lot, especially on holidays, when he was at home the whole day. He was suffering from constipation. At the ripe age of fifty-seven, which Indian male who likes spicy food does not suffer from constipation? Obviously, he will take more time to do the big job. What's the big deal? But this damn woman doesn't let him do it in peace! Irritable Bowel Syndrome combined with Irritated wife screaming! It's so bloody annoying.

But being an Aquarian, he has a rather calm personality. So, his anger subsided within no time. He tried to concentrate on tactics on how to off-load quickly, without any wear-n-tear caused to the most precious body part. Sitting on the ceramic throne, his mind slowly drifted from mundane biology to modern history, to his college days....

...It was his first day in college and he was getting late. Madras Christian College (MCC) is famous for its discipline, punctuality and studies. And some scandalous love stories, too. He didn't want to be hauled up the very first day itself. So, he hurriedly got down from the local train at Tambaram railway station and frantically started looking for an auto rickshaw. There were a number of autos but none was willing to go for such a short distance. Fed up, he started walking briskly, cursing all the auto drivers in this world with his collection of choicest Tamil abuses. Anyone within earshot, other than the auto drivers of course, would have definitely appreciated his vocabulary. It was indeed a connoisseur's collection!

Nearly halfway towards the college, suddenly

something shoved him from behind. He fell flat on the road face down. "You son of a bitch," he yelled and turned to face the culprit. His eyes fixed to his now horizontal body first spotted a pink scooty and then looking slightly upward, noticed and sized up its owner. Not a son-of-a-bitch, but a bitch, a good looking one at that, all by herself!

The culprit, a young woman still in her teens, hurriedly parked her scooty on the roadside and extended a helping hand to him. "Hope you are not hurt. I'm so sorry." She spoke in fluent Tamil while pulling him up from the ground. The uniqueness of Tamil Nadu is most of its native's penchant for idli, sambar, vada and general hatred of Hindi. With anybody and everybody, they always prefer speaking in Tamil; or at best in English. They can be seen shaking their heads and enjoying Hindi songs on their earphones while walking on the footpath or travelling in a local bus or train; but dare ask them something in Hindi and the majority will behave as if they have not understood the question and choose not to reply at all. Some might even ask you, "Tamil *terima*?" meaning 'Do you know Tamil?' And then and there, you are sorted, nice and proper!

The 'grounded' man was standing upright now. Being a Tamilian he had understood her. So, he smiled at her and nodded in the negative, suppressing all the pain and anger. He dusted himself, glanced at his wristwatch and started walking briskly. The woman shouted from behind, "It seems you are in a hurry. I'm going that way so can I drop you somewhere enroute?"

Janaki Raman looked back and hesitantly replied, "Today is the first day and I'm getting terribly late for my college."

"College? You mean MCC? Well, that's the only one around," she quipped.

"Yes, I presume," was his short reply.

"Oh! What a coincidence! I'm also going there. Today is the first day for me too. So why don't you just hop on behind me? Come on, let's go."

Reluctantly he sat behind her. As she picked up speed, he very cautiously tried to avoid any body contact with her. And he succeeded.

"I'm joining the BSc Pass course. Which stream are you in—BA, BSc or B Com?" she enquired.

"What a real coincidence once again, I'm in BSc too."

"Are you a local...I mean from Chennai itself?" she asked.

"Oh yeah! I'm from the airport area. How about you?"

By now their scooty was approaching the college parking lot. They ran towards their classroom and managed to overtake the lecturer who was about to enter the class. As there was no time, they both hurriedly occupied the only empty bench available at the rear.

"Well, boys and girls, a very good morning to you all. Way back in 1837, General Assembly School was founded in this very place by Rev John Anderson, a Scottish missionary. Nearly forty years later, on 1 January 1877 the institution was transformed and named Madras Christian College. You can Google to learn more about this famous seat of learning. I'm Prof Kaam Dev Lingraj, 'Kay Dee Sir' for you all from today. I will take your Physics classes. Now, please introduce yourselves one by one. Start from the front left corner."

OMG! What a funny name! It smells of sex all the way! Apt name for the Biology professor, not Physics. Almost everyone thought that way. But it being the very first session in the college, nobody dared to laugh out loudly. They all just exchanged silent smiles.

So, with complete sincerity, all tall, short, fat, slim, dark, fair, good, bad and ugly boys and girls started getting up one by one to blurt out their names and local addresses. At last, when their turn came, the scooty girl got up and introduced herself, "Hello all! I'm Janaki Devaiah. I'm from Tambaram itself and live just on the other side of the railway track and the state highway."

He was now completely taken back. What a damn coincidence this is! Anyway, as there was no time to be wasted, he stood up sheepishly and started speaking, "Good morning everybody. I'm from Meenambakam, staying in the Airport Authority of India housing colony. My name is Janaki Raman." He deliberately announced his name at the end, anticipating an uproar. And he was dead right!

The class could not take it any longer. Everyone burst out laughing. First it was 'Kaam Dev Lingaraj' and now 'Janaki and Janaki Raman' sitting together, that too on the very first day. What a joke this was! Even revered KD sir couldn't stop smiling.

What the hell? Janaki couldn't believe what she just heard. She looked absolutely puzzled and speechless. She looked at him intently. He is fairly tall, slightly dark and handsome. He also stared at her, rather nervously. He had that 'What can I do about it?' apologetic look. Such a coincidence in such a short span of time! Unbelievable.

Something stirred inside her. Maybe almighty God had actually destined them to meet this way. Maybe the roadside minor accident was also planned by God. She thought so. She smiled at him—the coy, 'Oh no, you have seen me without clothes last night' type of smile of a newlywed Indian bride to her husband the morning after their first night. He also started liking this dusky, beautiful and smart girl. It was love at first sight; technically, love at second sight for both of them!

Their unique but simple love story culminated in marriage six years later. Now Janu and Raman together have a son Jairam working in USA and daughter Gautami who was married off just a few months back in Coimbatore....

"You haven't finished yet! I know exactly what you are doing inside. That witch Shazida must have joined you. Having a great time together you rascal!" Janaki was up from her bed and at it once again. She now started banging the toilet door impatiently.

His mind came back from the thirty-year-old history to the present within a fraction of a second. Mind travels faster than light?

Raman quickly washed himself and got out. Janu peeped inside to catch Shazida red-handed, but there was no one to be found inside the toilet.

"You stupid woman! Where has that damn Shazida gone? Tell me now," he angrily inquired.

"Don't try to act smart with me. I know you have sent her out through the toilet window, haven't you?" She shouted back looking absolutely convinced.

Raman chose not to reply. There was no point. He silently headed for the kitchen. Today was Sunday. The maid won't turn up. So, he'll have to make breakfast for both of them.

He boiled one egg for his Janu and made a two-egg

omelette for himself. After preparing toasts he placed the tea pan on the gas. After a while the tea started boiling. And his mind too....

They had a picture-perfect family life till about six years ago. After leaving college Janaki had picked up a job in a private bank. Nowadays one's formal educational qualification doesn't hold any meaning in the job the person finally picks up. There are many M Techs who have become Investment Bankers, and MBBS doctors are joining the IAS in hordes.

He became a lecturer in a local college after doing M Sc and qualifying in NET. They had a simple, South Indian early morning temple wedding. Honeymoon? Simple too, in nearby hill station Munnar. There they had sex for the very first time. Then they had it all the time, for full three days, barring small breaks for eating food and answering nature's calls. They never went out for any other excursions! By the end of it, they had carried out threadbare analysis of each other's body. Thus, classmates became true soulmates!

Two years later Jairam was born. Still they both continued to work as their respective mothers took turns to look after the new born. However, after Gautami too came into their small world, Janaki volunteered to quit her job and become a full-time homemaker. Janaki Raman really appreciated it. Her job was a well-paid one.

Their days and years kept passing as expected, without any major issues and problems. Under Janaki's skilful guidance both the children were growing up well. And she was an extremely loving and caring wife too. Was she the best wife in the world? Well, he couldn't really comment on that as he hadn't seen other wives! But thanks to her devotion, he hadn't fallen in love with any beautiful young student in the college. Well, he never intended to. He, too, was a devoted husband!

Unfortunately, while crossing thirty-five, Janaki picked up Thyroid and Asthma as her other two independent lifelong partners. Nine years later, at the age of forty-four, she was diagnosed with early onset of Parkinson's disease. It happens to only one in two million! Very unfortunate indeed. And there is just no cure for this terrible disease. Medicines can only control the rate of growth, that too up to a certain extent. Janaki was depressed initially, but Raman and the kids, with all their love and dedication made her smile and come out of it within no time. With some restrictions, they were a happy family once again.

As the time passed, Parkinson's slowly started taking over Janaki's body and soul. Most of her physical actions and mental reactions were being controlled by the disease and the side-effects of the medicines she was taking regularly. Her movements became slower day by day.

While walking, albeit slowly, one of the legs would refuse to move suddenly, making her fall flat, face down. She became very irritable and also started losing track of time and space.

"Gautami, why are you going to college now? Today is Sunday, don't you remember?" She would genuinely ask her.

"No Mom, it's Wednesday today. Yesterday was Tuesday and we all went to the Hanuman temple in the evening. You've forgotten that already." Gautami would gently remind her.

Being a professor, Janaki Raman hardly travelled outside Chennai. So, before and after the college hours, he mostly made himself available to be with his beloved girlfriend turned wife. But one day he had to go to Hyderabad to attend a relative's wedding. The plan was to travel by train both ways and reach back home after three days. It was a deliberate plan to chill out and get a break from the monotony of his life. He had taken the evening train and reached Hyderabad by next morning. In South India, marriages are typically held in the morning hours followed by lunch. After enjoying a hearty meal, he decided to catch up on sleep. He had hardly slept in the noisy train the previous night.

"Hello Papa! Can you hear me? Mummy is not getting up since morning! She is unable to even recognise me. With help of our maid I've somehow managed to give her a bath and feed her something. I didn't want to disturb you during the wedding ceremony. I'm very scared Papa, please come back soon." Gautami's urgency jolted him back from his deep afternoon siesta. He could visualise his daughter's tearful face. Their bright son Jairam had already left for the USA for his MS course. Poor Gautami is all alone at home. He felt guilty and concerned.

After cancelling his train ticket for the next day, Raman took the earliest available flight to Chennai and reached back home late at night. Janaki was lying on the bed, semiconscious. He decided to change the doctor so took her to a well-known neurologist the next morning. "Hmm... you say she is suffering from Parkinson's for last ten years. What is surprising is that she hasn't started taking Syndopa tablets till now. The other medicines she is having are unable to work effectively any longer. It's high time we start with that." The elderly doctor was quite emphatic.

"Sorry doctor but my wife avoided this particular one thinking that it's a steroid," he said sheepishly.

"A little knowledge is always dangerous, you see. What she thinks has no base. As it is, does she have any choice left? If you don't change her medication right now, she will never come out of this vegetative state, that's for sure."

With the new doctor and new set of medicines, Janaki started improving slowly. She started going for small walks in the corridor adjoining their flat on the third floor of the society building. Her progress encouraged the neurologist to try some other new medicines as well, sincerely hoping that she would become fully fit once again. And of course, she responded very well. Within next six months she became quite energetic and started making numerous unaided rounds of their corridor through the day. This enabled her to lose nearly ten-twelve kilos as well.

But God only knows what happened thereafter. Things went haywire after about one year. She started seeing things and hearing voices which never existed. A visibly worried Raman consulted the doctor immediately. The doctor termed it as Hallucination, a definite and unavoidable side effect of advanced stage of Parkinson's disease. Doctors all over the world are known not to blame themselves ever for any mishap. In this case, too, the well-known neurologist of Chennai remained absolutely nonchalant, and never blamed himself for mishandling of the case, as he tried out all types of medicines on her, on the quiet.

After consulting with a few good friends and family members Raman took Janaki to a reputed psychiatrist, much against her wishes. The lady doctor prescribed some medicines to calm her down, and sleeping pills to ensure she did not suffer from insomnia; as it is believed that insomnia aggravates the case to a great extent. She also advised Janaki Raman and his other family members to always go the extra mile in order to comfort his beloved wife.

Persons who hallucinate always think that they are right and what they see is real. No amount of friendly advice and professional counselling can change their mindset. In Janaki's case also, similar thing happened. For some inexplicable reason she started believing that there existed a girl named 'Shazida'. She was just twenty-two years old, beautiful, married at an early age, mother of two young children, who was given triple talaq by her alcoholic husband recently. She lived and worked as a maid in the fourth floor flat just above Janaki's. Most importantly, her beloved husband Janaki Raman had fallen in love with Shazida! That damn female!

All hell literally broke loose in the Raman household. Earlier he had Gautami for moral support but after she got married, he was left alone, bravely fighting a losing battle.

The smell of burning tea brought him back to the present. Deep in his thoughts, he had forgotten to switch off the gas. He abandoned the half-burnt saucepan and quickly prepared two fresh cups of tea. Janaki was behaving near normal at the dining table. So, while patiently feeding her breakfast, he decided to bring back the topic of this morning's fight and sort out the issue once for all.

"Janu, when the maid is away, I give you a bath, change your clothes, feed you all the meals and even take you to the toilet. I care for you and love you so much. Why can't you just get rid of that imaginary character Shazida from your mind?" He gently but firmly put his argument across.

"What do you mean by 'imaginary'? How dare you? I've seen her waving at you when you left for office yesterday." She sounded dead sure.

"Come on darling! Have a heart! Shazida is nothing but your imagination as is your seeing her waving at me. Stop hallucinating, please!"

"Raman, I do understand everything. That Satan of a woman has surely done some black magic on you. And now you want to prove to the world that I'm hallucinating, that I'm mad. Then you'll throw me in some mental hospital and get married to her. Isn't it? You characterless fellow!"

Raman decided not to say anything further. Heavy doses of medicines and her weak mind were taking a toll of Janaki. She never spoke to him like this earlier. He felt bad for her and pity for himself.

Gautami, her husband Parikshit and his parents, Anubhav Rao and Anila landed up in the afternoon, unannounced. It was a godsent psychological relief for him. Raman liked Gautami's in-laws a lot. They were a mature and genuine couple, quite a rare commodity these days. Over lunch, while Janaki was sleeping, Raman told them everything about her mental state. The same evening while sipping tea, Anila started, "Janaki, why do you keep suspecting Raman of infidelity? He is a genuine guy and not a characterless man as you think. We are your well-wishers; you can't deny that fact. So when we tell you that you are hallucinating means actually you are! Please believe us! Make your mind strong; delete Shazida from your mind. That will make everyone's life easy, I swear."

"Anila trust me. I myself have seen her peeping through our window and heard her singing film songs just outside our flat. She really exists." Janaki wouldn't just let it go.

"But the other day when Raman left for the college you presumed that he had actually gone to meet Shazida, so you ran upstairs to catch him red-handed. But obviously you could not find him there; neither could you find that woman. In the bargain, you offended your neighbours very badly. What do you say about that?" It was Anubhav's turn this time.

Janaki gave a sarcastic smile, "It's so simple. They had hidden both of them inside the cupboard. That's it. Very clever neighbours we have!"

"But ma'am your neighbours have shifted in very

recently, and due to labour problems, the planned woodwork hasn't started in their flat. So they don't have any cupboard, really," exclaimed Anubhav.

Janaki shook her head in disagreement. Raman silently pleaded with Gautami's in-laws to end the discussion. It had reached the point of no return.

Janaki firmly believed in Shazida and her children's existence. The doctor treating her, her close relatives and even both her children tried many times to convince her but all of them failed miserably. She once told Gautami, "I know you and your brother are very skilfully sheltering your dad. Shame on both of you!"

"Come on Mom, you mean to say we actually want our father to get married to a twenty-two-year-old divorced maid, from some other community, who is nearly my age, and welcome her—I mean our new mother to our home with two small kids! This is absurd! Get your brain checked; there is some short circuit somewhere," a grossly agitated Gautami retorted and left her mother's bedside abruptly, angry to the core.

But Janaki remained unfazed. She always believed that Shazida was hovering around their house. She was also certain that whenever Raman went to the toilet, Shazida also got inside; and in there they did all kinds of dirty things together.

'She is in a dangerous stage now. She has a fear of

losing her love, her husband to a non-existing entity. You have got to be very cautious. She can even hurt herself," the doctor had opined once.

Keeping the doctor's warning in mind, Raman had been abandoning arguments half-way most of the time. He didn't wish Janu to get hurt in any way.

As a result, whenever he went to the toilet, she would stand outside trying to listen for any unusual sound. Whenever he went to college or to the local market, she would call him up a number of times and keep bothering him till he reached back home. It was all very annoying and disturbing. Raman was slowly losing his self-esteem and confidence!

Next morning Gautami and her newly acquired family left for a relative's house in nearby Puducherry. Handing over the home affairs to the old trusted maid, Raman also left for the college. After attending a day-long seminar he reached back home slightly late. Janaki looked very upset. She was quite sure that Raman had actually gone out on a date with Shazida. However, without getting into any argument, he quickly changed his dress and very patiently fed her dinner. After finishing his own food, he gave her water, medicines and very gently put her to bed.

"Raman, my dear love! Please don't leave me. I know how much you love that woman. I also know that she is young and very beautiful. You do one thing; I suggest you convert to Islam, get married to her and bring her to our house along with her two children. I'm absolutely okay with that, believe me!" Janaki started pleading with tearful eyes.

"Don't panic, I'll think about it later. It's going to be 11 pm, you should sleep now." Raman comforted her by caressing her hair casually. Within fifteen minutes she was fast asleep, clasping his hand close to her chest. After watching the news for some time, he switched off the TV, the lights and went to bed.

It was about 2 am. Janaki woke up hearing a strange noise. Someone was speaking in a hushed tone. She listened carefully in the semi-lit bedroom. After some intense and consistent eavesdropping, she could pinpoint the source of the sound. It was coming from Raman's side of the bed. She was now sure that Shazida had finally managed to enter their bedroom. How dare she?

She opened the bedroom door and tiptoed towards the kitchen. After switching on the lights and a little bit of searching, she got exactly what she wanted—a kitchen knife. She was going to teach that Shazida a lesson tonight. She was not going to leave her at any cost. Very slowly she tiptoed back to the bedroom. The window air conditioner was on and Raman was sleeping with a blanket over him. She approached his side of the bed cautiously. Janaki was sure that taking advantage of the darkness in their bedroom, Shazida had quietly slipped under Raman's blanket and was lying atop him enjoying! She can't let this happen, that too in her own bed, and in her very presence! She didn't want to give that terrible woman any chance to escape. Standing close to Raman's chest, she lifted both her shaky hands and brought down the recently sharpened, nine-inch long kitchen knife with full force. Nothing happened to Shazida. But with Janaki's vicious force, the kitchen knife went through Raman's heart and pierced the left atrium. As Janaki failed to balance herself against the recoil of her own action, she fell over the kitchen knife, almost immediately! That made the knife go deeper, through Janaki Raman's left ventricle too! Blood started oozing out like an uncontrollable fountain from his open chest. A jet of blood splattered over Janaki's face. Raman's body started shaking violently; it gave a final vicious jerk before becoming still. With that final jerk given by dying Raman's body, Janaki fell from his chest on to the floor still holding the kitchen knife tightly!

Gautami, along with her in-laws returned to Chennai by evening the next day. They pressed the bell a number of times but there was no response. They repeatedly banged the door; still there was no response from inside. Terribly worried and shaken up, they forcibly broke open the door. Raman was lying on the bed in a pool of dried blood, lifeless. Both his eyes were wide open, probably filled with fear and disbelief! Her mother Janaki was lying on the floor, the knife still in her hand! Her eyes were half open, looking at nothing. The room was stinking of urine and human excreta, both passed by her, unknowingly! She was heard softly murmuring… "Shazida, where did you vanish?" …once in a while! It was a pathetic, heart-wrenching sight!

Jairam flew in from USA two days later to perform their father's last rites. Unfortunately, their beloved mother had passed over the edge, completely unaware of what was happening around her. She probably had not realised that she herself had killed Janaki Raman! She did not even know that she had become a widow!

Janaki was immediately arrested but was later placed under police surveillance in the district mental hospital. In due course of time, first degree murder charges were framed against her by the local police. But based on her acute medical condition and past history of suffering from bouts of hallucinations, the criminal case filed against her was dropped by the Honourable Court. However, the court ordered her to be kept permanently quarantined in a bigger, better mental asylum. Since then Janaki has been kept confined in a secluded room in the govt mental hospital near Coimbatore, close to Gautami's house.

She visits her mother at least once a week. For obvious reasons, Jairam couldn't stay back in India for long. He will probably try his level best to return to India very soon and take up a job somewhere close by. He doesn't even mind a relatively low-paid job. Looking after his ailing mother is definitely more important.

Janaki looks pale and haggard. Her cheekbones have gained undue prominence in her otherwise beautiful face. She has almost stopped recognising her close relatives and own daughter. She is mostly seen sitting on the lone dining chair, engrossed in deep thought. Maybe in her own mind which, by now, has grossly degenerated due to the Parkinson's disease, she is still wondering, Where did Shazida go? How did she escape?

No one really knows if Hell and Heaven actually exist somewhere far beyond this materialistic world. But if that is so, Janaki Raman's soul will definitely be in Heaven. He must be looking at his beloved wife once in a while and feeling pity for her. By now he must have understood that it was her heavily medicated, foggy, unstable mind which actually killed him. She could never do any harm to her beloved husband!

She was such a loving wife, after all!

The Tip

"Hey Aditya! Where are you?" An anxious Pankaj was on the line.

Aditya doubtfully looked at his wristwatch. It was dutifully showing 11.37 am. And today was Tuesday. Then why the hell was Pankaj asking such a silly question?

"My dear, have you lost it? I'm in office, where else! And by the way, where are you? Not in your office, I presume."

"No, I am not. Aditya, do you know any good gynaecologist in our locality?" Pankaj sounded a little desperate.

"Why? What's the matter? Is Gita carrying again? Don't tell me! You already have two kids."

"Nothing of that sort." Pankaj ignored Aditya's jibe completely. "She has been going through some minor gynaecological problems recently. But today things have become somewhat critical. Do you know some good Doctor around?"

"Not really. Thankfully Sangeeta does not have such issues. But as you're saying it's a bit critical, I suggest you take her to a hospital straightaway. A bigger and better hospital where all tests can be done together easily and on the same day. Should I come along?" Aditya appeared concerned.

"Thanks for your advice, Buddy. I think I'll do that only. No need to come now. If needed I'll surely call you." Pankaj hurriedly hung up.

Aditya Khangura and Pankaj Gairola are old college mates. They both had done B Tech in IT from the same Engineering College in Rohtak. Then through campus placement they both got employed in the same company located in Jaipur and moved there. After a while Pankaj got married. Pankaj and his wife Gita have two kids. Their daughter Lina is 15 and son Ankush is 12 years old now. Aditya felt stupid for asking such a silly question about Gita's pregnancy but this type of leg pulling is considered okay between friends.

During Pankaj's wedding functions, Aditya came across Sangeeta, Gita's distant cousin. They had danced together in the Sangeet ceremony. They eventually fell in love and got married after about a year and a half. A few years later, Pankaj managed to get a better job and joined another company in Jaipur itself. However, they continued to live in same area and remained close friends. Almost eight years of marriage, after a series of scientific trials and unscientific tantric rituals, Aditya and Sangeeta were finally blessed with a baby girl. They fondly and aptly named her 'Pratiksha' meaning 'Waiting'. On the doctor's advice, they had decided to call it a day thereafter meaning no more trials, so no more kids.

Through his wife, Aditya was well aware that Gita was not keeping well those days, but he didn't know it was that serious. At middle age, most women go through some gynaecological issues, especially before menopause sets in. Anyway, he immediately called up Sangeeta. "Listen Baby, I think Gita has got some serious health issues. Finish your household chores fast and be ready to go to the hospital. They may require our help anytime. I'm going to be busy now so will call you later." Before she could fire a volley of questions, he ended the call abruptly.

Aditya actually got busy with usual conferences and other office work and nearly forgot about Gita. On his way back, he suddenly remembered. He quickly dialled his wife again, "Hey Sweetie! Did you call them? What's the latest?" Depending on his mood, Aditya called her by many names—Baby, Sweetie, Janu or Luv.

"I have been calling both of them but no contact. Both mobiles are apparently switched off. Don't know what's going on!" Sangita sounded worried.

"Don't worry. Get ready quickly. I'll pick you up shortly and go to their house. Get little Miss Pratiksha also dressed up." Seeing a traffic policeman standing just a little ahead of him, he ended the call immediately.

Aditya and family reached Pankaj's flat by 6.30 pm. They found Lina and Ankush in the house looking terribly worried. Both their parents were missing.

"Where are your Mom-Dad? Why have they switched off their phones?" he enquired.

Lina couldn't control herself any more. The poor girl broke down in Sangeeta's arms. In between sobs she spoke, "Uncle, Papa has taken Mummy to Rajasthan Hospital. He called me two hours ago and said they were taking her to the OT for a big operation. I don't know what's wrong with her. Papa didn't tell me anything else. He must be still in the hospital. He had said mobiles couldn't be kept switched on inside. I am so scared!" She continued to sob.

"Just don't worry dear. Nothing will happen to your mom. You both come and stay at our place till the time your parents reach back home." He and Sangeeta helped them to quickly pack their essential items and set course for their home. After safely depositing all of them at home Aditya left for the hospital immediately.

He couldn't find Pankaj anywhere in the hospital compound; neither could he find Gita. Worried, he approached the Duty Nurse at the small Reception of the Operation Theatre to enquire. As usual, a petite Keralite was on duty. Most Keralite men set off for the Gulf countries as unskilled or semi-skilled labourers. Most of us may not know that the regular Air India flight operating between Trivandrum and Dubai is jokingly called 'Kerala Express'! Similarly, most Malayali women set course to various parts of the country as nurses. They are found everywhere in large numbers—be it Srinagar in the North, Kanyakumari in the South, Jamnagar in the West or far off Itanagar, the capital city of Arunachal Pradesh. They are a sincere, dedicated and professional lot. As expected, she first ascertained his credentials and relationship with the patient. Then, with her heavily accented English, she slowly and deliberately started her monologue in a nasal voice. "Your sister-in-law Gita was first examined by the Gynaecologist at the OPD thoroughly. She was immediately referred for an urgent ultrasound test. The ultrasound showed the presence of a big cyst in her abdomen. So, our on-duty surgeon immediately called up the Oncologist. They both talked for five minutes and decided to operate on her and remove the cyst without wasting time. I myself was inside, as part of the operating team. Believe me, we all were so shocked to find a huge lump 'Thees Beegg' (she prolonged the words and simultaneously cupped both hands to indicate the approximate size). It had grown so much that it had affected the stomach also. I mean, part of her large and small intestines! That's why the surgeon removed her ovaries and the affected portions of both the intestines as well. Luckily, the whole tricky and long operation was successful. The Oncologist is suspecting that the removed lump is most probably malignant. So, we have simply handed it over to your friend for getting the biopsy done as quickly as possible at the Government Hospital. Please pray and hope that it doesn't come out to be malignant, otherwise she will be in 'beeg' problem!"

Aditya was stunned. He well understood the hidden meaning of her last word. It was a shocking revelation. God help Gita! He silently prayed for her and thanked the nurse profusely.

Gita had already been shifted to the ICU. She was still not in her proper senses. So, he decided to wait outside the ICU for Pankaj to come back. Pankaj returned only after 10 pm. He looked completely shattered. Aditya comforted him and forced him to have dinner in the hospital canteen. He also deliberately avoided asking him why his mobile phone was not kept on. As the biopsy report would be available only after a few days and no one was allowed to visit or stay near the patients admitted in the ICU, they decided to go back home and get some well-deserved rest.

Gita started progressing very well. After two days she was shifted out of the ICU to the General Ward. The much-awaited biopsy report came after three long days. It was like a thunderbolt from a clear blue sky. As initially suspected by the Oncologist, it was indeed malignant! After a few further tests the final verdict was pronounced. Forty-one-year-old Gita was suffering from Stage 3 of Ovarian Cancer. And 'Cancer' has no 'Answer'.

The life of all the family members of both Gairola and Khangura families changed overnight. Gita was shell-shocked. It was a herculean task for others to inspire and talk her out of the present state and save her from associated acute depression. Chemotherapy was also started in earnest. Whenever Gita had to visit the hospital for the chemo and needed complete isolation thereafter, for a day or two, Sangeeta brought the children home and took good care of them.

Time passed quite slowly and painfully for all of them. After successfully undergoing all the scheduled chemotherapy, Gita definitely felt better and more cheerful. She slowly tried to get her own life and that of her other three family members on track. Her cousin Sangeeta and her jovial husband Aditya stood like rock-solid pillars with them. Things around both the families were becoming better with smiles appearing on their faces. Gita finally accepted Ovarian Cancer as her unwelcome guest and got used to living with it. Pankaj had also gone back to his work. He loved his wife and both the children but he loved his work too!

It was nearly a year since Gita's major operation. Things had become near-normal. But suddenly one night she woke up with terrible pain in the stomach. It was 3.30 am. She did have light but bearable pain for last two days which she was ignoring. Actually, she had not passed stool for three days in a row, and without consulting the doctor she consumed a fair quantity of laxatives. But that too didn't help. Alarmed at her pathetic state, Pankaj called up Aditya immediately. Aditya came with Sangeeta and Pratiksha, dropped them at Pankaj's place and took Gita and Pankaj in his car to the same hospital without any delay.

Gita was immediately hospitalised but she had to suffer for another half-a-day with agonising pain as the doctors tried various medicines to diffuse it. Unsuccessful, they then decided to cut open her stomach to find the root cause. The outcome was unbelievable. When they had operated on her the first time, they were forced to remove affected parts of the large and small intestines. They then re-joined the shortened intestines.

But somehow the passage between the two had got blocked completely, causing unbearable discomfort to the patient. So now they reopened the joint and refixed it after a thorough clean up. While doing so, the surgeon noticed a small lump mushrooming near the old spot! It was very alarming!

After the patching up was done, a semi-conscious Gita was wheeled into the ICU. The Oncologist called Pankaj to his OPD chamber. As Pankaj occupied the chair in front of him, the doctor started his monologue. "See Mr Pankaj, I've just operated on your wife. What I found was that the usual passage between the two intestines had got narrowed down considerably. That severely restricted the flow of the entire food and water intake she had in the last couple of days. Another two to three hours delay would have cost us very dearly as her intestines would have burst. Anyway, things are okay only as of now…."

Pankaj opened his mouth to ask something but the middle-aged, bald but handsome doctor raised his hand. The doctor continued, "Why I said 'as of now' is because I've found a small lump in that area which had caused the blockage. This one has come up too soon. Very unfortunate but the truth is, you have to become very strong now Mr Pankaj."

"What exactly do you mean by that, doctor?" Pankaj was sweating, though the outside temperature was just

19 degrees celsius. It was a cool March morning in Jaipur.

"I'm really very sorry Mr Pankaj but it's a case of relapse, an early relapse. Things are not looking bright at all. If you wish, please take a second opinion from some other Oncologist. But I must warn you now, she doesn't have much time. She really doesn't!" The Doctor stopped his monologue abruptly. He looked tired and unhappy with himself.

Pankaj felt as if he was drowning, drowning in the Dead Sea! No, you actually can't drown in the Dead Sea because of its very high salt content. He was drowning in the Sea of the Dead!

"Oh my God! How much time?" He could barely speak.

"I can't quantify exactly. Maybe a few months, maybe six, maybe one year. Nothing more than that I suppose. Unfortunately, she has very quickly progressed to the very last stage. I suggest you keep her at home for better care and monitoring. Do things to keep her happy, always. If possible, take her out on a well-planned holiday, maybe with family and friends. Whether to break the news to her or not, well, I leave it to you."

Pankaj shook hands with the doctor and left the chamber, still in a comatose frame of mind. Everything around him appeared blurred and revolving.

Aditya was the first one to whom he broke the terrible

news. It gave him an ugly, hollow feeling inside. Aditya was equally shocked. Gita has just crossed forty. This is no age to die, he thought to himself.

After a week-long hospitalisation, when Gita was declared fit enough to leave, she was discharged and driven back home. Pankaj had confided in and consulted all his close relatives and friends in the meanwhile. Almost all of them opined that at an opportune time the bad news must be broken to Gita.

As per plan, Gita's humble, old and ailing parents slowly broke the unpleasant news to her the same evening. It was done just after the evening tea and in the presence of the entire family. Quite naturally, Aditya, Sangeeta and Pratiksha were also present in the room. Gita just couldn't digest the news. Keeping her head on her frail mother's shoulder, she just cried and cried. Everyone cried in silence too. It was terrible!

Gita almost continuously cried, felt pity for herself and her young age, cursed God for her plight and sobbed through the night. No one stopped her from cursing God; no one even tried to console or silence her. As planned earlier, they just left her to come to terms all by herself.

By next morning, she had somewhat controlled herself. She understood very well that nothing but a miracle could stop her from dying within a year. Being educated and well-bred, she now asked God for forgiveness for the curses showered on him the previous night. She hugged her two lovely children and then she signalled her beloved husband and whispered her last wish. "You keep visiting foreign countries on official tours so often but I've never been abroad. So, if you can, please take me on a small tour to some inexpensive country close by. And take me there before I die! Please!"

Poor Pankaj, who was somehow trying to control himself so far, hurriedly put his right index finger on her lips to quieten her but he himself broke down on her slender shoulders.

Thailand is close by and not a very costly country to visit but people say the country is more popular and famous for sex-tourism. Pankaj wanted to take his immediate family on a vacation together. So, Thailand was ruled out by him. After a lot of browsing of numerous tours and travels websites and free consultations with knowledgeable friends, he finally selected Bali, the Indonesian hotspot. It was decided that they would go after a few months, in October, when the temperature was comfortable there.

Keeping Gita's state of health in mind he also decided not to book any conducted tours. Those were so cramped time wise. Also she wouldn't be able to travel in buses and in groups for sightseeing. Therefore, he looked for the cheapest air tickets and comfortable budget hotels and resorts at Bali. A thorough web churning threw up a hotel next to the beach for a very reasonable amount. It also showed that Air Asia was providing the cheapest flight options.

On coming to know of the reasonable ticket and hotel costs, Sangeeta coaxed, coerced, blackmailed and threatened poor Aditya to join the gang. The very next day Aditya expressed his desire to take his own small family also to Bali. Gita and Pankaj welcomed the proposal with open arms. In fact, they felt very happy and indebted to Aditya for becoming part of the group. Finally, the hotel rooms were booked and return tickets were purchased for all seven of them. The flight was scheduled to depart Delhi at around 11 pm and reach Bali around 1 pm (local time) the next afternoon, with two and a half hours layover at Kuala Lumpur, Malaysia. As the journey date kept coming closer, Gita's excitement grew in leaps and bounds and her suffering reduced considerably.

Finally, the D day arrived one fine morning. Though the doctor had advised they carry a wheelchair, both Pankaj and Aditya decided against it. They had thoroughly searched the internet and found that free wheelchair facilities were available at all the airports and hotels.

They had hired a Toyota Innova and set course from Jaipur in time in order to reach Delhi airport by 8 pm.

Enroute, they stopped at the Midway Tourist Resort run by the state-owned RTDC at Behror. While having tea, Pankaj received a worrisome message on his mobile phone; it read, 'Because of some technical problem the flight departure time has been postponed to 4 am tomorrow morning'. At that stage they were actually half way to Delhi. So, it was not considered prudent to go back all the way to Jaipur. They just decided to continue towards Delhi at a rather slow speed. They finally reached the international departure terminal of Indira Gandhi International Airport by 9 pm. As anticipated, a wheelchair was arranged for Gita by the airline staff immediately.

The Air Asia flight finally took off from Delhi at around 5 am and landed at Kuala Lumpur after four hours, around 11.30 am local time. It was a bright sunny morning. The airline staff at IGI Airport had already sent a 'Request wheelchair on landing' message to their handling staff there. So, when a visibly excited Gita deboarded the aeroplane, she was met by a tall, darkish, lanky man on the aerobridge itself. "Namaste Madam! Welcome to Malaysia." He bowed perfectly before putting her in the wheelchair very gently.

Gita, a first-timer in foreign tours, never expected an Indian there. "Are you an Indian, really?" she asked. She did not know that thousands of Tamilians had migrated to Malaysia hundreds of years ago and settled down there. Majority of their descendants who have never visited their motherland are gainfully employed today, but unfortunately most of them are unskilled or semi-skilled labourers.

"I'm Gunasekharan, a Tamilian by origin. My great grandfather came here from India almost a century ago. Now I'm a Malaysian citizen by birth." He slowly started wheeling her towards the Airlines Transit Passengers Facilitation Centre. His footsteps were almost literally followed by Gairola and Khangura family members. Because of the delayed arrival from Delhi they had obviously missed the connecting flight. The airlines staff apologised profusely and accommodated all of them on the next flight to Bali.

"What about their food coupons?" Gunasekharan demanded. Pankaj and Aditya had no clue what Mr Gunasekharan was talking about. But before either one of them could open their mouths for a clarification, the airline staff on the desk spoke up, "Oh sorry! Yes, of course! Here they are." He took out seven coupons and gave them to Guna who handed them over to Pankaj saying, "Your flight was delayed by the airline because of which you all missed the connecting flight to Bali. So, as a compensatory measure they have to give you food vouchers during transit halts. These coupons are worth

20 RMs (Malaysian Ringgits) each."

It was like sweet music to their ears. They all started looking around for a suitable restaurant. Guna advised, "The Food Court is upstairs, on the first floor. But most of the outlets serve local cuisines. Those dishes being spicy may not be very palatable for you, especially for Madam. So, I sincerely suggest you dine in the Burger King." As per the local time it was approaching lunchtime. They were feeling hungry too. So, they nodded their heads in agreement.

Before having food, Gita wanted to visit the washroom. So Guna dutifully took her to the toilet meant for persons with special needs. Both Sangeeta and Lina helped her. Everyone suddenly felt the urge to visit the toilets. Inside the Men's toilet, Aditya went towards the loo and Pankaj headed straight for one of the cubicles for the big job. Actually, he had tried to do it in-flight but failed.

In the absence of any hand-jet, Pankaj used the toilet paper roll quite liberally. Satisfied, he got up. Lo and Behold! There were a lot of coins kept on top of the paper roll holder! He stopped, picked up the coins and had a closer look. Surprisingly, all the coins were of one Ringgit each. He counted; in all there were 12 Ringgits. Now he understood. Every guy who used this toilet to relieve himself had dutifully left one or two coins as tip for the sweeper on duty. But why hasn't the sweeper picked these up? There are so many of them. He scratched his brains for a probable answer. He suddenly remembered the beggars in India, begging outside the temples and at traffic junctions; their begging bowls always had some coins and were never empty. It never crossed his mind but now he realised it was a simple but effective marketing strategy!

Pankaj felt a little embarrassed at not being able to leave any tip for the on-duty sweeper, whoever he was. He quickly joined the gang waiting outside for his return. Guna then wheeled Gita through the circular, transparent lift to the Burger King outlet located on the first floor. There was a big queue, mainly of visiting and transiting foreigners. Guna managed to find a table and six vacant chairs for the group. After parking and locking Gita's wheelchair he made a serious announcement. "Your next flight will depart after two and a half hours from Terminal 2. Presently we are in Terminal 1. We have to take the connecting driverless train to reach Terminal 2. But as you've already got the boarding passes, I will come back here after one and half hours to fetch you all. Till then please enjoy your meals." He left, probably for a quiet lunch in a remote corner.

Pankaj, Aditya and Lina stood in the queue while Sangeeta and the two younger ones stayed back with Gita for company. The coupons were good enough to buy sumptuous meals for all of them. Everybody really relished the chicken burgers, French fries and cold drinks. Pankaj was a fast eater so he finished the meal rather quickly, much ahead of all others. He was thinking about something very seriously. At IGI Airport he had given Rs 100 as tip to the guy who had dutifully carried Gita in the wheelchair right up to the aeroplane door. Here his country-cousin Gunasekharan was doing so much for them with selfless devotion. He must give him a generous tip. But how? He didn't have any local currency. None of them had. They were carrying plenty of Indonesian rupiah and US dollars. Rupiah has no value here. But yes, he could give some dollars to Guna. US dollars are normally honoured everywhere but the lowest denomination he had was a 20 dollar bill. So, he decided to ask Aditya. "Yaar I must give a tip to this gentleman, Mr Gunasekharan. But I've a 20 dollar note. How about you? Can you please spare me five dollars? We will square up later."

Aditya was munching finger chips dipped in white sauce. He licked his fingers and took out his wallet. Unfortunately, the lowest bill he carried was a 50 dollar one. He showed that to Pankaj, who looked dismayed.

"Firstly, there is no need to give any tip to Mr Gunasekharan. He gets paid by the airline for the services he is providing to us. But if you still insist, I suggest you go to the Currency Exchange counter downstairs. Out of the 20 dollar note get only 5 dollars changed to Ringgits; rest of the money you take back in USD. As per today's rate you will get four Ringgits per dollar. That means you'll get 20 Ringgits by changing 5 dollars. You can give him 10 Ringgits now and keep the rest for tipping during the return journey."

"Oh! That's an excellent idea, Aditya. I'm proud of you Bro! Five dollars will be Rupees 350 approximately. That means I'll give 175 Rupees to Gunasekharan now; that's fair enough. Thanks, I must pay him that. His good wishes will be good for Gita," Pankaj replied and immediately left for the Bank outlet located on the ground floor.

He approached the window waving the 20 USD note. "Can you please change only five dollars in RM? The remaining amount I want back in USD only. I'm a transit passenger and need only this amount," he pleaded with the young woman seated across the counter.

"I do understand you, Sir. But as per our government rule we cannot change any foreign currency in part. I have to change the whole note and give you Ringgits only. That will be 82 RMs. Are you interested?" The woman asked in a polite tone.

"No…no. Please try to understand my plight!" Pankaj sounded desperate.

"Sorry Sir, I can't help you. Next gentleman, please!"

The lady clearly didn't wish to entertain him any further.

Pankaj felt absolutely helpless. Like how he had felt when the Oncologist delivered his final verdict on Gita. What could he do now? It's a fact that he did not know Gunasekharan till half an hour back. But the way this man had been helping them out definitely fell beyond the call of his duty. Above all, he had made Gita happy. Her smiles meant a lot to him. So, come what may, he would give this man a generous tip before leaving Kuala Lumpur. But how would he manage that? Should he exchange full 20 dollars into RMs? But in that case what would he do with all those extra Ringgits? Those probably couldn't be used in Bali. Pankaj was thinking rapidly. For Gita's treatment, he needed money now, and a lot of it! So, he couldn't just waste money unnecessarily.

Unmindfully he started going towards the toilet. As he entered, he realised that this was the same toilet he had visited an hour ago. Suddenly, the picture of those coins casually kept by individual donors, above the paper roll holder, flashed in his mind. Oh yes! Here it is. He immediately decided the next course of action. Pankaj quickly entered the same lavatory he had used earlier. To his good luck, the coins were still there. He picked up all the coins and briskly counted. The total had gone up to 14 Ringgits. Pankaj briefly whispered 'sorry' to the faceless, unknown sweeper, before quickly pocketing ten coins. While exiting the main door, he breezed past a middle-aged, nearly bald man in navy-blue uniform. He smiled and saluted Pankaj smartly. Pankaj glanced back. The sweeper! Oh shit!! He nearly ran out.

At the restaurant he found everyone had finished their lunch and had been waiting for his return to move to Terminal 2. Aditya looked at him with inquiring eyes. Pankaj just showed a 'thumbs up'. Aditya relaxed. Guna arrived after a while and smilingly wheeled Gita out. The short train journey was thoroughly enjoyed by all the three kids. They were amazed to watch how it worked. At Terminal 2, they headed for the aerobridge to board the flight to Bali. After Gita got down from the wheelchair, Pankaj thanked Gunasekharan and handed over ten Ringgits. Guna took the coins hesitantly and thanked him many times. "God bless you, Madam! Get well soon," he said to Gita before disappearing into the milling crowd.

Pankaj heaved a sigh of relief. He had achieved his aim. He had made Guna happy, very happy. But somewhere in a little corner of his mind he felt guilty, guilty of theft, and of cheating; cheating an already marginalised, poor sweeper. How could he do such a lowly thing? Shame on him!

The holidays at Bali went off exceedingly well. All of them just freaked out. Gita, his beloved wife, was on cloud nine. Seven long days just flew by. Pankaj enjoyed himself, too, but somehow his guilt never left him alone. The very first day in Bali he had gone to the local money changers to enquire. There he had found out that Malaysian Ringgits could easily be exchanged for Indonesian Rupiahs. That meant he could have got full twenty dollars converted into Ringgits and tipped Guna from his own money, not from stolen money. And to top it all, he wouldn't have lost any money unnecessarily! The guilt started growing inside him with each passing day. He started spending sleepless nights on his otherwise comfortable hotel bed.

His extreme sense of generosity slowly gave way to acute depression. And the worst part was he couldn't share it with anyone. Not even with his best friend Aditya. But Pankaj had to somehow come out of it for the sake of his family. More importantly, for Gita's sake. His mind was in turmoil looking for an answer, a good answer, a workable solution to calm his mind.

Returning from a well-enjoyed holiday is always a sad affair. Everyone was generally very quiet on the return flight from Bali to Kuala Lumpur. Gita was put in a wheelchair not by Guna but another man of Malaysian origin. Mr Gunasekharan was off-duty. There was a two-hour transit halt again. As both the flights were on schedule, there were no free lunch coupons. And none of them wished to have lunch as it was not lunch time either.

They were taken from Terminal 2 to Terminal 1 by the same driverless train. There Pankaj excused himself and quickly headed for the toilet, the same one. He hurriedly entered the same cubicle. He went straight towards the paper roll holder. It had only two coins placed on a square tissue paper with something scribbled on it in capital letters. He bent down to read. It read, "I POOR MAN". He felt terribly ashamed of himself. He must be the sole cause for this! This small chit amply clarified the fact to him that the same sweeper, the same poor man was on duty, once again!

Pankaj took out the coins and turned the tissue paper upside down. He took out a pen and wrote on it 'SORRY' in fairly big capital letters. He then slowly put his right hand in his pocket and brought out 20 RM coins kept wrapped in a paper. Just a day before departure, he had got some Indonesian Rupiah changed into Ringgits, thirty RMs to be exact. He had lost some money in the process but didn't really mind it.

He placed all wrapped twenty coins over the tissue paper, and placed the two coins on top. That made a total of 22 Ringgits. He wanted the sweeper on duty to know, to realise and understand his compulsions. He would give the remaining 10 Ringgits to Gita's wheelchair handler as tip while leaving this country. Fully satisfied, he left the toilet to join the group. Fortunately, there was no 'close encounter of any kind' with the sweeper this time around!

The Air Asia flight lifted off for Delhi after an hour. Pankaj sincerely hoped that by now the toilet cleaner had got his money back, doubled in a week. He felt happy and contented with himself. 'Pankaj' in Sanskrit means Lotus. It also means 'Born out of Mud'. Yes, he belonged to a humble but cultured middle-class family. And though he had faltered a week ago, today he had finally lived up to the meaning of 'Pankaj'. He did not let his own, his family's and his country's name down in any way.

For the first time in seven days, Pankaj fell asleep almost immediately after take-off. He slept very peacefully throughout the four and half hours long flight, with a shy, happy smile on his face.

Four months later, Gita left for her heavenly abode one night. She expired in her sleep, with both hands folded over her chest and a beautiful, happy smile on her lips. People say most cancer patients have a slow and painful death as all the major organs start failing one by one. Everybody's good wishes were with her. Maybe those and her own Karma ensured that she did not suffer at all.

Pankaj had prepared himself and the kids for this unavoidable eventuality. Life has to go on, people have to move on. He has to bring up their children single-handedly now, filling the huge void left by his beloved wife. Should he get married once again, purely for physical intimacy, for his bodily pleasures? No way! He just doesn't want to complicate his children's lives, that too at such a tender age. Gita's fond memories are good enough to see him through for the rest of the journey called 'life'. Well, whatever little is left of it!

21.12.2112

Shahrukh Khan sat on the SHIT pot to relieve himself with the CREEP put over his head. The SHIT (Smart Hi-fi Interactive Toilet) is the latest, most popular technological innovation by mankind. When you sit upon it, it automatically but quite gently grips your posterior and lets go only after you have finished and pressed the 'Off My Butt' button. Depending on the final quantity and consistency of your download, its built-in computer decides on the type of wash you are entitled to, namely 'Gentle/ Moderate/ Strong'. Also, based on the prevailing climatic conditions it automatically takes a call on Hot or Cold wash and also between Soapy or Just water wash. Well, surprised! Don't be! Because this is the Twenty Second century Babes!

This is the fourth course of action in his unwritten

list of daily morning chores which Shahrukh has been following very religiously for last thirty-five years or so.

The first chore of the morning–Gulp down a small cup of a crazy-tasting juice called 'Amritam' immediately after waking up. Taking inspiration from 'Sagar-Manthan' mentioned in our ageless Puranas, a German scientist named Ambitious Curious invented this supertonic just a decade ago. Amritam is made of various herbs, aloe-vera juice, extremely small portions of single malt scotch, xxx white rum, Russian vodka, Indian toddy and some selected sea-weeds crushed into a liquid. This is an elixir of life in true sense, created to prolong human life to a minimum of 150 years. And the die-hard consumers are actually living beyond that. Well, Shahrukh is only 96 now. It's really a long way to go for 150! Forget about that, he is still four years away from becoming a Senior Citizen of the country. And there are men who are still producing children at his age!

Just the other day, his 91-year-old friend Salman Khan, and his 78-year-old wife Latrina Rauf had invited him and Gauri to his seven-year-old son Salala's birthday party. There his dear friend narrated an interesting story. Just a few days ago, Salman Khan was asked by his son as to how he was born! In reply, he had explained the entire thing quite technically. He said, "Well son, one day your Mom and Dad connected on Facebook and became friends. Then your Dad sent a Tweet inviting your Mom to visit a particular Cybercafé. There we found out that we had many likes and links in common and that we actually understood each other very well. When we both were not on laptop, we would chat on WhatsApp and Skype. And we both were dishing out more and more likes to each other. Then, one day we decided to share our files. So, your Dad introduced his USB stick to Mom's USB port. But only after the files were downloaded, we realised that we had actually forgotten the relevant security software and that we had no firewall or snapshot filter in place. And it was really too late to cancel the entire download. It was also impossible to delete the files generating the message 'Installation Successful'. Soon after this, your Mom's monthly notifications stopped coming. Finally, nine months later, 'You' appeared as a New User Contact, requesting for Login and Password." And Salala understood it all!

The second chore–Do 'CANDY' for next half-an-hour. This is the newest form of light dancercise. CANDY is the very latest, prudent scientific mixture of Cardio exercises, Neolithic dance and our own desi yoga. Almost everyone living in and around this world does this at home regularly. Yes, you heard it right. 'Around the world' because it includes thousands of our own people residing on the Moon and Mars permanently.

The third one–Have a cup of herbal tea with Gauri, his 89-year-old wife. The tea is prepared by Kalpana, the Romaid, their household robotic maid. He really relishes the bed tea in a half-lying, 'Sleeping Buddha' posture while resting his left shoulder on his favourite cylinder-shaped organic side-pillow.

And the fourth chore is to head for the toilet ten to fifteen minutes later, when the pressure becomes unbearable and things are ready for getting offloaded. It is like the bursting pressure inside a cooker, ready to come out with full force and with a lot of noise! And surprisingly, the process of relieving himself mostly follows the pressure cooker pattern. In case of a cooker, after the initial noisy outburst the gas is generally reduced to 'Sim', making the subsequent releases somewhat tapered, prolonged and less noisy.

Similarly, he also takes nearly 15-20 minutes to complete this particular morning routine. He utilises this private, leisurely time to go through the CREEP, to gen-up on the universe and about things happening around. CREEP is the short form of Cinematic Realtime Everything on Earth Presenter, a recent invention, a one-piece global replacement for the century-old wall mounted TVs, Laptops, Tablets and the I-Pads. It's a 7D Head-set, which works as a super laptop, interactive video-newspaper and presents both live and deferred

Reality TV shows, live telecast of sports events, latest movies and much more. It actually resembles a cyclist's helmet with sunglasses, a slightly bigger one at that. Its glasses can be either normal or powered, progressive or bifocal, plain or polaroid. It's made of Mlastic, a good mix of metal and plastic which makes it extremely light. It's HUD (Head Up Display) allows the CREEP to be used like normal spectacles while walking or driving. It works on pocket size batteries and can also be used for all functions of a laptop by using registered voice commands. No more cumbersome typing! And lastly, at home it can easily be plugged into a large monitor/TV screen for group viewing, as a home theatre.

Today is 21 December 2112. By 2112 Hrs tonight, that is at 9.12 pm, the world will end! Unbelievable but true. Rather, going to be true. This is what the scientists and the CREEP reports are harping on for the past one year. God knows how and why but they have definitely managed to create a hype. And the pitch is rising day by day. But why should the world get destroyed by this date and time? No one really knows. Reports say that almost a hundred years back, the world was believed to get wiped out by 21.12.2012. The logic? That particular date was regarded as the end date of a 5,126 year-long cycle in the Mesoamerican Long Count calendar, popularly known as the Mayan calendar. Though Mayans never wrote about total destruction, but it was propagated to be so. Things literally had reached a crescendo on that date. But fortunately, nothing happened. The world and all the mortal inhabitants lived on. And that's how Shahrukh, born 96 years back in 2016, is still alive.

Fortunately, this time around, no old civilisation was dragged in. Some years back, a few astronomers and many astrologers across the world predicted that some heavenly object would fall on the earth today. The meteorite, the so-called impending disaster has been nicknamed 'OSAMA'. But why today and at this particular time only? Is it because of the sheer peculiarity of it? 21.12.2112; 2112 Hrs? Maybe those propagators of this dicey theory just took a fancy to this unique combination. Also, it has been exactly a century from the previous 'Date with Destiny'. And in these 100 years, technology has advanced so much that the warning can't just be ignored. But whatever it is, if it actually comes true, all will be dead tonight. Period!

Nonchalant, he started browsing through all the related news articles. Most were centred upon the impending disaster. The editorial page had chronologically deliberated on all major events that happened in the world in last 100 years. Being an old history student, he decided to concentrate on the past events. What's the point of thinking about what would happen if the end actually came! Well, all will die, what else? He is nearing Senior Citizenship (100 years of age). At this juncture he is not scared of death. Moreover, instantaneous death is always the most welcome one. So why waste your precious time bothering about it?

CREEP continued to play the major news events one by one, giving Shahrukh enough time to go through it completely. It presents clippings at a speed depending on the hooked-up reader's age, educational qualification and current mental agility. And the unique 7D presentation by itself is awesome! So, Shahrukh continued browsing. The listing of chronological events of the century gone by interested him the most.

2019 AD–In India, the NDA (BJP and its allies) managed to win the General Election once again, surprisingly with a much better margin than the previous one. NDA secured total 354 seats against 272 required for a simple majority. INC definitely fared better than 2014 elections by securing 54 seats, no thanks to the Gandhi scion! However, the much publicised opportunistic Mahagathbandhan went through a bitter divorce during the honeymoon period itself. Shri Narendra Modi got a second term as PM. As expected, long term financial reforms continued. But, to everyone's surprise, the govt soon carried out what is famously called, 'A surgical strike on the bureaucracy', to hasten up the much-needed reforms in IAS and IPS and other allied cadres of govt administration.

2020 AD–Infamous COVID 19 took its toll. More than one million people lost their precious lives across the world. Due to his quirky policies and mishandling of the pandemic, Donald Trump and his Republican party lost the general election in the USA to the Democrats with a huge margin.

2021 AD–Mrs Michelle Obama of the Democratic Party took oath as the first woman President of USA. The Afghanistan problem got nearly sorted out by her deft 'Look Asia Policy', and as a fallout, ISI led Pakistan was politically embarrassed globally.

2022 AD–First Bullet Train started operating between Mumbai and Ahmedabad in India. ISIS was finally wiped out completely with joint effort by the US led NATO forces—the Russian, Indian and very surprisingly, the Chinese forces!

2023 AD–A big news from the neighbouring terror-haven! Pakistan finally faced the much-anticipated economic disaster after she was officially declared a confirmed bankrupt nation by the IMF. Her lopsided policy of secretly diverting foreign funds meant for internal development towards creating disturbances in neighbouring India and Afghanistan, and also for instigating and patronising dormant Islamic fundamentalists in China, sealed Pakistan's fate at last. Mighty China, the Sleeping Dragon, their friend for last two decades, was in complete shock initially. The Chinese immediately went all out to punish Pakistan for the daring misadventure and the terrible backstabbing. Pakistan was internationally forced to neutralise all nuclear weapons and related facilities; and also made to destroy all terror camps and training centres completely, in full public view. They were immensely pressurised to give back POK to India unconditionally and free Baluchistan completely. Baluchistan was declared the youngest independent nation (196th) by the UNO. China finally realised its strategic mistake and made India their ally. The near-prehistorical nationwide dream of 'Akhand-Bharat' finally came true. What an achievement for all of us proud Indians!

2024 AD–A historic resolution was passed in the UNO whereby India was declared the sixth permanent member of the most prestigious UNSC, United Nation's Security Council. Now onwards, along with USA, UK, Russia, China and France, India would also enjoy the exclusive right of using the Veto. India has truly become a world player!

2025 AD–Here comes the funniest and at the same time the most useful news item of this century. As per the epic Mahabharata, Draupadi was specially blessed by

God to regain her virginity after every sexual encounter so that she could satisfy each one of her five legally married husbands! Taking cue and inspiration from this story, an Indian scientist couple, settled in the USA, has managed to develop a Combo, a tonic for sipping and a special Gel for internal use by women. These ensure that a woman continues to remain a virgin, well, nearly one! A Tamil Brahmin scientist named Shri Mahalingam and his equally bright wife Orally Amma have taken pains to find a suitable name for his unique product too, 'Vagino-Moto'. This has changed the entire outlook towards sex, worldwide! Men and women are so happy now. Fresh feeling each night, every time! The sales graph of this product has bypassed all expectations.

2026 AD–Under Narendra Modi's able guidance and active involvement, India was declared a Cashless Economy. Ninety-nine per cent of India's financial transactions will now onwards be by electronic or other means of transfers. Remaining one per cent will be by cash, but limited to Rupees 100 per transaction only. Subsequently all currency notes of bigger denominations were bought back in a planned, phased manner by the government.

2027—A technological innovation has now made it possible to get post-mortem of a human body done without any cuts whatsoever.

2028 AD–With commercial satellites becoming increasingly cheaper to launch, operate and maintain, all mobile service providers across the globe finally got rid of cumbersome tower-based services and changed over to satellites. This benefitted the end users immensely as mobile connectivity became possible in each and every remote corner of the world. Seamless video calls from Alaska to Antarctica became a reality. It also ensured that all types of roaming charges, domestic as well as costly international ones, were permanently withdrawn by all operators across the globe.

2029 AD–Breaking news of the century! China, the very last bastion of the communists, finally fell flat on its face! And almost like erstwhile USSR, China too got divided into a number of smaller states, sorry, independent nations. Pakistan's prolonged covert operations to instigate the minorities in China paid off at last, as the Uyghurs, the major Muslim community, created their own country, Uyghuristan. Tibet also got her long overdue freedom. Taipei, Hong Kong too gained their independence. Now, there are a total of 206 independent countries in the world. Along with such political disaster, the Chinese financial dominance, the much anticipated infamous bubble also burst. Phut! There goes the superpower, for good! But China per se still has the right to Veto.

2030 AD–Historic first contact was established with people living in other solar systems. The exoplanet named 'Alpha Centauri C', situated nearly 4.5 Light Years away, beamed back reply signals sent by NASA. So, we are not alone in this universe! What a relief!

2031 AD–The most spectacular achievement was made in Meteorological science this year. Technology was developed to capture lightning and convert and store it as electricity for use in immediate future. Technology to convert cyclonic storms, typhoons and tornados into useful rains was also mastered. This has finally put a worldwide end to catastrophe caused by such extreme weather phenomena.

2032 AD–With advent of Microcells like the microchips, all vehicles all over the world, except the military ones, were compulsorily changed over to battery driven only. The batteries could get charged easily by the super solar panels fitted on the outer body of the vehicle, thereby making it commercially and operationally viable. Fossil fuel usage saw a drastic decline all over the world. Hence dominance of petrol producing nations took a severe beating too. A well-deserved beating, isn't it!

2033 AD–Global warming, though reduced considerably since last decade, finally took its toll. All glaciers in and around the polar caps and the majestic Himalayas melted completely. This resulted in rise of sea level by three and a half feet, submerging most of the low-lying areas of Norway and Bangladesh. About 90 per cent of the islands of Maldives and Indonesia and majority of those located in the Pacific Ocean region too got usurped by the unforgiving, gigantic sea. Saddest natural disaster of the century, indeed!

2034 AD—'UNO approved' commercial mass production of 'Labourer Robots' was finally started in Japan. They were meant purely for domestic use only. The 'Romaid' was made in both female and male (for use in some Islamic countries) forms, with fully developed yet non-reactive sex organs. This was deliberately done to avoid any kind of untoward sexual abuse at home. Later in the same year, in order to cater for unprecedented demand, Japan opened a licensed production facility in India too. At the time of purchase, the buyer needs to give a specific name to the Romaid which will be accordingly registered with the govt agency. And in future the Romaid will respond only when called by that particular name. Well, Shahrukh and Gauri have named their Romaid 'Kalpana', after the human version of it (technologically speaking) who dedicatedly served their household for 27 long years before finally signing off from this world due to old age.

2035 AD–Purely lab-grown synthetic human organs got patented and approved by the WHO. These will henceforth replace any and all unserviceable parts of a human body. Though a little expensive, this option has become the biggest ever boon in healthcare industry the world over till date. Probably, except some genetic defaults and terminal cancer which get detected much later, all other ailments have become fully curable now. Periodical servicing of human bodies, somewhat like car servicing, with immediate faulty part replacement facilities was started in some developed countries.

2036 AD–Colonisation of Moon and Mars became a reality as the first two batches of 500 volunteers left for their destinations this year, for good! Science has nearly reached its pinnacle, literally.

2039 AD–Exactly 100 years after the Second World War had started, World War III engulfed the entire globe once again. As correctly predicted by famous soothsayer Nostradamus, this one was started by a green-turbaned Asian religious leader-cum dictator. Religion was never the root cause behind the previous two world wars. But this time around, religious fervour took its toll quite early and very aggressively. Majority of the nations got embroiled within no time. By concerted efforts put in by some prominent world figures, global ceasefire was effected within four months. But by then, twenty-three big cities were reduced to ashes and the world lost more than two billion people, thereby reducing the total population by nearly twenty-five per cent. What a manmade disaster!

2040 AD–Most of the nations had successfully switched over to cashless economy before the third world war. And now, with the world population drastically reduced and the global economy reaching its lowest ebb, the IMF, the newly emerged all-powerful global financial body has unanimously decided to have just one global currency. Accordingly, three most widely circulated and most popular currencies were shortlisted. Out of those three, one was finally voted as the 'Global Currency'. Dollar, what else!

Shahrukh Khan suddenly felt a massive jolt. He nearly got thrown off his throne, the SHIT. It is still morning, he is damn sure. Then, what the hell? Has that much talked about, written and discussed about heavenly body with 'helly intentions', meteorite OSAMA finally hit the Earth? His entire body shook once again, this time more violently. Shahrukh Khan now screamed his heart out in terrible fear....

"Come on Shomu, get up! It's 8 o'clock now. You have to reach office by 9.30. You have a client meeting at 10 am. You forgot! How can you sleep so much?" Garima, Shomu's wife was shaking him vigorously.

Shomu aka Shoumen Chatterjee of Durgapur, West Bengal, was startled. He jumped up from the bed sweating profusely. Oh my God! Bed? But he was in the toilet! Wasn't he? Wasn't he sitting on the SHIT commode with CREEP around his head? He looked up at the digital clock hanging on the opposite wall. It showed 8.06 am, Tuesday, 15 Jan 2019, 23*C. Oh God! Today happens to be their elder daughter Ankita's birthday. He has to get back home early and take the family out for dinner.

What were all those things then? Shoumen got up from the bed and rushed to the toilet to finish off the morning chores at a fast pace. Sitting on the commode he started wondering about last night…

Himself, 96-year-old Shahrukh Khan, his wife Garima – Gauri! He is a die-hard fan and an avid admirer of superstar Shahrukh Khan. That meant in his dream last night, he himself had become Shahrukh! How very funny! And Garima had automatically become Gauri Khan! And what about all those other crazy things? SHIT (Smart Hi-fi Interactive Toilet! What the hell!), CREEP, Meteorite OSAMA (What?), life enhancing Amritam, CANDY (Cardio exercises, Neolithic dance and desi yoga!), Michelle Obama–the first female president of USA (What imagination. She has not even announced her candidature yet!), Cashless India, Vagino-Moto (Oh my God! really?), India's UNSC membership and Veto power, bankrupt Pakistan, Uyghuristan, free Tibet, Chinese bubble burst, Planet Alpha Centauri C, microcells, Romaid (their own 55-year-old maid Kalpana is very much alive and washing utensils in their kitchen right now), synthetic organs, colonisation of Mars, World War III, Dollar, the single global currency and most importantly, 21.12.2112? Were all those things nothing but a part of his dream! Just a dream! Oh! Jai Ma Kali!

Now he clearly remembers. Last night he had typical Bengali food—boiled rice and egg curry for dinner. And then Garima forced him to have the third egg from her own share of two, that too much against his wishes. He now suddenly recollected that when he was a child, his Bengali mother used to say and remind them all, 'If you ever eat more than two eggs at night, in any form, your stomach will soon get bloated up like a balloon and you will definitely have nightmares'. And mothers are never wrong! Specially the Bong mothers!

So, to surmise it all, he had had a bad dream, more appropriately put, a nightmare last night. It was definitely the craziest dream one could ever have! Uri baba!

Freedom @ Midnight

Benita loved Shillong. She was born here but not in the heart of this beautiful town. Like many others, she is from its outskirts. She hails from a small village near Five Miles.

Shillong was a favourite hill station of the British officers posted in and around the states of North East India. As per their then prevailing standards and maybe some typical localised personal requirements, the distance from the city centre to various scenic but remote places was measured in miles. And to simplify things for the innocent locals, the authorities generally made a bus stop at the end of each mile. Over a period of time, small little villages came up on hill tops around these bus stops.

Miss Benita Marbaniang is her full name. Like thousands of children born in progressive modern India every day, she is also a mixed breed. Her mother is a local Christian Khasi. Her Hindu father is a Marwari trader from Jhalawar, a dusty backward town in far-off Rajasthan. These Rajasthani traders are a very enterprising lot. They are found in every nook and corner of this country, be it Rameswaram in Tamil Nadu, Srinagar in Jammu and Kashmir or Mokokchung in far off Nagaland. And the best part is, where one Marwari goes, several others follow suit soon. Her father Rajeev Lakhtakia had landed up here in the early seventies and started a small venture. Within a year he fell in love with Monica, a local tribal girl and got married to her in typical Khasi style. Khasi tribe, till date, is essentially a matrilineal society. So, after the marriage Mr Lakhtakia moved into his wife's house. It suited him fine as he could now save the rent of his flat and commute daily to his workplace by the typical low roof buses. Benita was born after two years.

Being the only child, she grew up as a quiet girl, introvert in nature. Her parents being from two different parts of the country, from two distinctly different cultures and moreover from two different faiths, had nothing much in common, except love for each other. But as the years passed, the physical and mental gap widened and love also diminished between the two progressively. By the time she finished her schooling and took admission in St Mary's College, her father left the household and the town, for good. With not many friends to speak to and hang around with, Benita automatically became very close to her lonely mother Monica.

"Mom! Why did you marry Dad? There was nothing common between you two. So why?" She once genuinely enquired.

"Love is blind, my darling! And not only blind, it is deaf, dumb and mentally challenged too! We just fell in love and got married. That's all. Maybe there is nothing known as love. It is only the external, physical attraction. And because of this crazy attraction, you tend to ignore all other ifs and buts. So, my child, don't ever commit this mistake of falling in love. You will ruin your life!" Monica dished out a crisp sermon. Benita smiled and nodded. She was nineteen now and yet to find a suitable boy, yet to fall in love.

With plenty of tribal genes in her body and soul, she loved the hills, the forest—anything scenic, natural or wild. She enjoyed boating in the Ward's Lake and chasing colourful butterflies in the famous St Anthony's Botanical Garden. Whenever she managed a break from boring college lectures, Benita either visited one of these places or just went on small treks in the nearby forests, mostly alone. Love for nature had also given rise to some artistic creativity within her. She loved reading books related to wildlife and on India's freedom struggle. Out of many she read, she particularly liked one book, *Freedom at Midnight* written jointly by Dominic Lapierre and Larry Collins. God only knew if her liking was because of the sheer powerful content of the book or just because it was published in 1975, the year of her birth! She didn't know. If and when in a good mood, she penned one odd poem casually. Fortunately, one of her small poems titled *Freedom at Last* got published in the college magazine. It was loosely based on political happenings around 1947, finally leading to India's independence on 15 August 1947. She earned instant, though short-lived celebrity status in the college overnight. Whenever alone, she preferred humming it very softly, for her own ears only.

One sunny afternoon in December she was enjoying a boat ride in the picturesque Ward's Lake, rowing all by herself and humming her favourite creation. Being all alone in the boat she was doing it rather loudly this time. She had nearly reached the centre of the lake. Suddenly, glancing behind she realised that another boat was following hers, though very slowly. There were no other boats floating nearby from whom she could ask for help. She felt alarmed. The boat came very close and stopped. A young man was rowing it. He looked at her and smiled, "Hi! I'm Captain Alex Bonix. Sorry for following you like this. I know it's very improper but I heard you reciting a beautiful poem so could not resist myself. Who has written that poem?"

All signs of fear disappeared from her mind; a pleasant smile appeared on her face instead. She felt happy and elated. Though a born introvert, she just stepped out of her cocoon.

"Hello Captain! I'm Benita, Miss Benita Marbaniang. Nice to meet you. I don't know if it's a beautiful one or not, but yes, I've written it. Thanks for the compliment, anyway." She extended her hand spontaneously across the boat for a shake. The firm hand of an Indian army officer gripped her slender one. A pleasurable shiver went down her spine. She could suddenly feel a thousand butterflies fluttering inside her stomach. On his part, the young Captain continued to hold her hand, shaking it for a fairly long time. And she did not mind it at all! Their actions were pointing at mutual attraction, instant liking for each other.

Capt Bonix, a bachelor boy, originally belonged to Kerala and was posted to Jorhat in neighbouring Assam. He had come to Shillong, 'The Scotland of the East', on a short holiday. Their mutual attraction soon blossomed into a full-fledged love affair, the very first one for both of them. He went back to Jorhat the next weekend. They continued to communicate with each other mostly through letters. After more than a year of long-distance courtship they decided to take the next step, to get married. Benita being very close to her mother decided to break the news first, before Alex could come and formally seek her hand from Monica, his would-be mother-in-law.

"Mom, I wish to tell you something. I'm seeing someone." Benita started without much of an introduction.

"Benita, please don't tell me you've fallen in love with some outsider. Don't tell me that you have also become a blind woman like me, please!" Monica's voice showed instant anger.

"Yes Mom. You are right. I like Captain Bonix a lot. He is in the army, now posted to Jorhat. He wishes to come and ask you for my hand. Being in a transferable job, after marriage he wants me to move to Kottayam in Kerala to live with his aged parents. He is their only child, you see. He gets two months leave every year; he will visit us then. And this arrangement is quite okay with me, Mom."

"My dear child! For heaven's sake, don't repeat my mistakes! We Khasis live in a matrilineal society. In our tribe, the husband moves into the house of the newly-wed bride. And the ancestral properties get transferred to the eldest daughter of the family. Our entire family properties are with me right now. If you get married to someone from outside and move out of our household after marrying him, all these will automatically slip out of your hands. And God forbid, if your marriage breaks down after a few years, you, my poor child will be on the streets, literally. I can't let that happen. Oh my God, I can't just take it at all!" Monica spoke forcefully with genuine tears in her eyes.

"But Mom, I'm well educated and independent. In case of any mishap in future, I'm sure I'll be able to take care of myself. So please don't worry on that aspect," Benita insisted.

"Benita, my dear! Listen to me very carefully. My childhood friend Noerma from nearby Sasruk village visited me the other day. You remember her very well, don't you?"

"Yes, I do somewhat. But so what?" Benita shot back.

"Well, Noerma seems to like you a lot. She is very keen to make you her daughter-in-law. She doesn't have any daughter. So as per our customs, after the marriage she will adopt you as her daughter and you will own all her ancestral properties as well. You know it very well that her late father was the Chieftain of their big village; he owned a lot of fertile land and plenty of pigs. And the best part is, after the wedding you won't have to move out of this house; your husband Kiang will move in here instead."

"Kiang! That High School dropout, that drunkard, who when not high on booze, chews pieces of betel nut? I don't wish to marry him. No way!"

"Which Khasi man doesn't drink these days, tell

me! And presenting others with Tambul and chewing it once in a while is our custom. Please be practical in life, darling. Think of the huge properties you are going to inherit. And do believe me, for fear of losing it all, Kiang will not be able to leave you. And if at all anything happens to him, financially you need not worry a bit. Am I making some sense or not?"

"Marriage is not a matter of compromise; it is of choice, Mom! It happens only once in our lives. I'm very keen on leading a good life and am not interested in land and pigs!" Benita sounded adamant.

"Benita, will you actually leave this lonely old mother of yours, all alone here to fend for herself! And that too for a man about whose family you know nothing, just nothing at all! You can't speak a single word in Malayalam. And we don't even know if his parents can speak in English or Hindi at all. In that case, how will you communicate with each other? By sign language? How will you live with them? And what will happen to me once you go away? You won't be able to visit this old lady every year. I will die a depressingly slow and lonely death. Maybe that is the last wish of Lord Jesus for me," a desperate and crying Monica fired her masterpiece salvo amply spiced with typical Indian emotional blackmail. It hit the Bull's eye! It had to!

Benita had nothing to counter-attack with. She stared

at the teary eyes of her middle-aged, beautiful, divorced mother and just surrendered, unconditionally.

So, rich and spoilt boy Kiang Kharluki, Class 11 failed (two attempts), got married to Benita Marbaniang, MA (English) in a befitting Khasi wedding ceremony two months later. Maintaining the centuries old custom, Kiang moved into Benita's home. After a few months she was customarily adopted as daughter by Noerma. Then Benita moved into her mother-in-law's house permanently, with Kiang in tow. Monica was left alone at her own home now, though not very far away.

Initially her married life went smoothly. Benita really tried a lot but could never forget her first love. And Kiang was not a great lover. They did not enjoy each other's company much; but he had sobered down a lot. He opened a small utility shop near the bus stop. After nearly two and a half years Benita gave birth to a baby boy. He was named Yangdo. As time progressed, Benita got more and more involved and engrossed in bringing up the child. As it happens with most first time mothers, she started ignoring Kiang and his needs. That made him lose focus from the business sooner than expected. And probably as a compensatory measure, he quickly revived his drinking and Tambul eating habits. His penchant and capacity for both started increasing exponentially with time.

After another year, Noerma, Kiang's loving widowed

mother, though just fifty-seven years old, suffered a sudden and massive heart attack while having a bath. She fell flat and, in the process, kicked the bucket, literally. Quite unfortunately the century-old English Idiom was played out by her, though unintentionally, while finally departing this world.

Benita now officially inherited all the properties hitherto held by her beloved mother-in-law. All agricultural and rental incomes started coming to her on a regular basis. Kiang had become totally incomeless on the other hand, fully dependent on Benita's patronage. As in a matrilineal society the mother runs the entire family and also takes care of the children, Benita soon had her hands full. But she continued to dole out the same amount, as was earlier decided by Noerma, to her hubby as pocket money every week.

But Kiang was not at all happy with this arrangement. He started demanding more money as his drinking had increased considerably. Benita didn't want her young husband to become an alcoholic, like many of his friends around. Her steadfast refusal to part with more money to sponsor his binging led to frequent quarrels initially. But when quarrelling didn't fetch him more money, he resorted to abusing and beating her up badly.

Kiang was stout and five feet three inches tall, fairly good height as per Khasi standards. Benita, on the other hand, measured up a little short of five feet and was very slender, no match to Kiang. So, like most other Indian women subjected to domestic violence, she had to bear it all, always and every time.

"You stupid bitch! Give me half the money you earn every month, or I'll beat you and your son to death," he said once while slapping her. By now concerned about her son's safety and equally scared about her own, she reluctantly doubled his pocket money the next week. But he managed to finish it off within just four days.

One night he came back home heavily sozzled. "Benita, you bastard of a female! You Motherf....You've taken over all my properties. Now listen you bitch! Sell off all my mother's assets and give me half the money you get. Then you can move back to your God damned mother's home for all I care. Take Yangdo along. He is your responsibility now! And if you want, I'll sign the divorce papers and set you free, but only after I get my share. Do you understand, you idiot?" He started abusing and beating her mercilessly. Hearing his mother's screams, one-year-old Yangdo felt scared and soon joined the family chorus, a mixture of screaming and crying. It was very unpleasant!

"Mom, you had advised me to be practical in life but you've actually ruined my life. I'm not yet thirty and what do I have to look forward to in life? Responsibility of a young child and an abusive, drunkard husband who beats me black and blue every night! And then he forces himself on me, abuses my womanhood too! I think I'm pregnant again! Is this what you call a marriage? The so-called oldest surviving institution in the world! My foot!" Benita sounded dejected and angry.

Monica was on a monthly visit to her daughter's home. She knew all about Kiang's changed nature. She also knew that of late he had been secretly visiting a married but separated woman living in an adjacent village. Benita apparently didn't know about it and Monica decided not to tell her. Why unnecessarily burden the child further?

"Dear girl! I think you should be more patient. Show more love and affection towards him. Make him feel wanted. I'm sure he will come around soon," Monica said.

"Oh mother! How very funny you're sounding. Every night he comes back home heavily drunk and abuses me with the choicest ones, thrashes me up badly, then forcefully has sex, at times unnatural one, and after that starts snoring almost immediately. And you want me to wake him up early morning, plant kisses on his swollen cheeks and whisper, 'I love you sweetheart! Can I get you tea and a few biscuits? Or would you like to have some Vodka?" Benita spoke to her mother in a very rude and sarcastic way.

"Okay then please tell me your plans. How are you

going to tackle this?" Monica genuinely enquired.

"I don't know Mom but I'm really getting fed up! How I wish I had listened to my heart and not succumbed to your emotional blackmail. Come what may, Captain Alex wouldn't have turned out to be a wife-beater," Benita spoke from her heart.

"Let anything happen, I'm not going to sell any property just to make him happy," Benita continued. "Recently I read somewhere that an Indian Punjabi woman in England had tied up and set her alcoholic, tyrannical husband afire. One fine night I might do the same. I feel so helpless and insulted."

"Please darling! Don't ever think on such lines. What will happen to your Yangdo when you get sentenced to ten or fifteen years in jail? Who will take care of him? Yes, of course I will. But what will happen after my death? And what will happen to you as such after you come out of the prison? Will you be able to live a normal life thereafter? Come on, tell me!" Monica asked logical questions.

"Maybe you're right this time. Frankly, I'm also not inclined to spend the rest of my life in jail. But what do I do with him, Mom?" Benita sounded very worried.

"I'll speak to all his close friends tomorrow. Let's see if they can influence him to change. As of now, please enjoy your tea and pork rice. And let me relish it too."

Monica did speak with some of his very close friends the next day but most of them were his partners in crime. So, none of them were forthcoming in helping Benita. Monica felt dejected. So Benita continued to be subjected to physical and mental torture meted out by her husband. Her sheer helplessness and anger were making her extremely edgy. She was reaching the boiling point, the breaking point.

It was 13th August, a Friday. It had been raining cats and dogs since morning. One of those terrible, bad weather days. As usual Kiang had left home after lunch, with an umbrella and a 500 Rupee note forcibly snatched from Benita. He got back well past 10 pm, very badly drunk. Benita had already fed Yangdo his little semi-solid dinner and dutifully put him to bed. She was now braving herself for the impending physical and mental onslaught.

"Benita, my characterless wife! When will you sell off my mother's properties? You bloody whore! You don't like sleeping with me, hey! Because you love sleeping with that pig boy-friend of yours. Yeah, Bonix is his name, isn't it? By the way, whose son is Yangdo? Mine, or his? Come on, tell me the truth!" Kiang started abusing and thrashing her with his bare, burly hands.

Benita was dumbfounded. How did he know about her secret and sacred affair with dear Alex? But whatever it is, he can't drag our son into it. She felt terribly pained. She couldn't take this nonsense anymore. She must fight back, now!

Benita mustered up all her courage, jumped up to land a tight slap on his cheek and shouted, "You earthworm! How dare you speak to me like that?"

He had never expected such an assault from his otherwise submissive, meek wife. He stumbled and fell flat on the ground. Benita took her sleeping son on her lap, sat down in the corner and started sobbing. A heavily sozzled Kiang got back his bearings slowly, got up and caught hold of one of his leather belts. He suddenly attacked her with the belt from behind. Extremely infuriated, he continued to shower her with filthy abuses while beating her with the belt mercilessly and dishing out occasional kicks. Benita hugged her child and took the entire brunt on herself. Kiang stopped beating only after he felt completely drained out. Benita had cuts all over her body and she was bleeding from many spots. She somehow managed to get up and walk off to the bedroom, hugging the baby tightly. She was not crying anymore. She just wanted to escape from this endless torture, leave everything and run away to Alex; if not, at least to her mother. But it was pouring very heavily outside. She had to wait till the rain stopped or at least till the morning. It was dangerous to step out now.

Extremely tired, disgusted with life and terribly hungry, Benita soon slept off cuddling her dear son.

All of a sudden Benita woke up with a jolt. In the semi-lit bedroom, she could make out that she was no longer sleeping on the bed. She was lying in the narrow space between her side of the bed and the wall. Who had thrown her off the bed? Kiang? But then where was that bastard of a monster now? And where was dear Yangdo? She quickly rubbed her sleepy eyes and tried to reach for the baby, presumably lying in the middle of the bed. As she managed to catch Yangdo's hand, the room started shaking violently once again. She almost lost the grip on her son. Oh my God! It's an earthquake! And a massive one at that! Holding the baby very tightly against her trembling chest, she tried to look around in order to take stock of the situation.

The entire house was still shaking, though mildly now. She couldn't get any glimpse of Kiang. She suddenly felt quite weak and hungry. She realised that she actually had not eaten anything since a cup of tea and two biscuits at five in the evening. She somehow struggled and managed to climb back on to the bed. Benita then rolled over and got down from the other side. With the help of intermittent lightning outside, she found the switchboard and tried switching on the lights. But surprisingly only the night lamp came on. Though it had been pouring the whole day and now at night they were experiencing an earthquake, fortunately the electricity was not disconnected. The main light might have got fused due to the quake, she presumed.

In the dim light, she could easily scan the entire bedroom. What she saw was horrifying. Part of the roof, luckily towards their feet, had nearly collapsed. A major part of it had already fallen on the floor and a big chunk was hanging and swaying, very precariously. But there was no sign of Kiang. Had he left the house and run away when the quake started? Extremely tired, hungry and her mouth dry with fear and thirst, she slowly started searching for the torch. Kiang or no Kiang, she must leave the house immediately.

"You Brotherf… stop pretending as if you haven't seen me. I'm trapped under this rubble. I can't move my legs. Come and rescue me. Come on, you damn daughter of a witch," Kiang's abusive, commanding voice terrified her.

Benita looked towards the source of the sound. She found Kiang half-seated on the floor near the wall. Both his legs were lying awkwardly bent outwards under a huge chunk of cement fallen from the roof. She could see a lot of blood splattered under the chunk. He appeared completely immobile and in terrible pain. But, how did he reach there? She was thrown off the bed, understood. Little Yangdo was probably sleeping in between the two of them, so he remained there. But how did that monster land up near the toilet! He was terribly drunk. Maybe he had gone there to puke and at that time the earthquake struck. Anyway, how did it matter now? She had to decide on her next course of action, fast, real fast.

'So what if he abuses and beats you every night! So what if he has beaten you up very badly this very evening too! That too with a leather belt? He is your husband after all. You must save him at any cost. Come on! Be a good, obedient wife!' Her good inner soul spoke up.

'So what if he is your husband! He is a demon in human form. This is the best opportunity to get rid of him forever. Come on Benita! Go ahead. Just do it!' The very next moment Benita's bad inner soul screamed from within.

Both her good and bad souls kept screaming inside her head, turn by turn. She felt terribly tormented, unsure of what to do.

She was undecided. She tried to collect herself and get up. Last night's severe thrashing with the leather belt had left many sores on her body. Her whole body hurt. She was terribly hungry too. She somehow managed to get up and then headed straight for the kitchen. Luckily the door was not jammed. She quickly grabbed and ate two bananas and drank a glass of cold milk without sugar. Then she grabbed an apple and went back to the bedroom. Kiang was still abusing her continuously at the top of his coarse voice. Benita picked up her son and tied him up on her back with a shawl, typical Khasi style. Young, innocent Yangdo now looked like a small backpack, his small hands dangling in front of his mom's shoulders and his equally small head peeping from behind her slender neck.

The earth shook again, very violently this time. The hanging chunk of roof shook too. It now appeared dangerously close to Kiang, just about two or three feet above him. He screamed again in dire panic, "You stupid whore! Hurry up and take me out of here now. If I catch you, I'll bury you alive. I swear on my dead mother, you bitch!"

His shrill curse and abuses were like the last nail in the coffin. Benita took her long-awaited decision immediately. She looked around and within no time picked up the homemade snake catcher kept behind the entrance door. It was a strong, longish stick made of pinewood and is found in almost every household in the village. Snake menace is quite rampant in this area. She quickly went near the hanging chunk of cement to judge it properly. Then she faced Kiang and gave him a hard, cold look, which was quickly followed by a sinister smile. For the first time in his life, Kiang appeared scared, mortally scared. "What the hell are you going to do? Why are you staring at me like that, you bloody bitch!" He now screamed in a trembling voice.

Benita gripped the stick firmly with both the hands. Concentrating all her energy, she swung the stick like a cricket bat, almost like the famous Helicopter shot of MS Dhoni, to dislodge the cement chunk till now precariously hanging over Kiang's head!

A terrified Kiang screamed at the top of his voice, "Oh no! What the ...."

All of a sudden, the shrieking stopped abruptly. There was a deathly silence in the room. The huge chunk had fallen down with a heavy thud, bang on the intended target—Kiang's head. It had broken his skull into two uneven pieces! In the dim light of the night lamp, it was a ghastly scene to watch! Benita turned her face quickly, trying to control throwing up!

With her son on her back, she swiftly headed for the exit door of the house. She briefly looked at the wall clock mounted above the bedroom door while finally leaving the house. It showed 1.20 am. It was early morning on 14 August. An Indian housewife had finally earned her well-deserved independence from her tyrannical husband and from a dreadful marriage on the Pakistani Independence Day. Freedom @ Midnight!

Benita went out of the house. She had a sad smile on her face. She could not have taken the risk of staying inside any longer. God knows when the next round of quake would strike! The rain had stopped briefly. She sat under a pine tree and started thinking about herself, her life and also started contemplating her next move. Though not in touch since her marriage to Kiang, she would try to contact Captain Bonix once again, maybe tomorrow itself. If needed, she would go down to Jorhat all the way to look for him. His good friends in his army unit would definitely help her out to find his latest address and the new contact number. If he was still unmarried, he might accept her, you never know! She must give it a try, a sincere and dedicated try to bring her life back on track. She knew that Captain Bonix had loved her a lot and would not turn her away. She was a damn fool to choose Kiang! Damn my Mom!

What she did not know was that one fateful night a few years back, Captain Bonix had gone out with his small team of soldiers for patrolling the designated area outside their highly fortified camp. Somewhere enroute, the separatist ultras had laid a trap and waited. His entire team got trapped and subsequently ambushed by the terrorists in the wee hours of night. Without fearing for their lives, they all fought back valiantly. After an hour long fierce battle, Captain Bonix managed to kill three extremists but in the bargain, his own body was riddled with four bullets. An hour later, he breathed his last on the operating table of Jorhat Air Force Hospital. He made the supreme sacrifice for his motherland. This happened just about four months after Benita's hurried, unplanned marriage to Kiang.

Captain Alex Bonix of the Indian army died an unsung hero. Quite dejected with life after she had rejected him, he just didn't wish to live any longer, anyway!

Doctor-Doctor

"Hello! Can you hear me? Who is speaking?"

"Well, now the time is half past one. And being the middle of the night, the date has also rolled over to the next one. And you've dialled Ashfaq's mobile number! So, it is understood that obviously Ashfaq only will speak. By the way, who the hell are you calling me at such a comfortable time?" A visibly agitated Ashfaq spoke up sarcastically.

"Mr Ashfaq, I'm Senior Nurse Rita calling from the Emergency Ward, yes, from the Government Hospital, Tezpur. Zikra Khan, your sister, has been admitted here just a while ago. She is quite serious. Can you come over? Yes, at the earliest, please." The dutiful, beautiful nurse replied in a rather serious tone, ignoring his sarcasm completely.

"What the hell? What happened to her? Has she delivered the baby?" Ashfaq sat up on the bed jolted out of his sleep. Zikra was nearly eight months pregnant with her second baby he knew. But how could she deliver so early? Still a month to go!

"No, not really. It's much more complicated than that. But I can't explain things on phone so I suggest you reach the hospital as soon as you can. It is very urgent." Rita, the nurse hung up abruptly. She had lots of other more important jobs to do as well.

Thanks to a forward looking, progressive India, even the remotest villages including 'Kuchi Muchi' are now well connected by roads, electricity and of course, mobile network. So, he immediately rang up Barkatullah Khan, his brother-in-law, to find out the details of Zikra's sudden sickness. But the recorded voice echoed in his ears, 'the number you have dialled has been switched off, try later,' in Assamese, English and Hindi, in proper, pre-decided sequence. What's the matter? Why is his mobile off at this crucial time? Has the battery got discharged fully? And why hadn't Barkat given him a call before admitting Zikra in the hospital? Or just after admitting? Ashfaq got worried now. He must leave for Tezpur without wasting any more time.

His sister, now around twenty-three, has been married to Barkatullah for the last three years. They have a cute two-year-old daughter named Mehr. Zikra's husband is a middle level state govt employee in Tezpur. They live quite happily in their own small house on the outskirts of the town. Happily? Well, that's what he had thought till now.

Ashfaq reached Tezpur Govt Hospital by nine o'clock next morning. By then Zikra had been shifted from the Emergency Ward to the Female Ward. Ashfaq walked straight in to see his ailing sister. But, as expected, it being a non-visiting hour, he was not allowed to enter the ward. Instead, the Duty Nurse called him to her office.

"Hello Sister! How's my sister now? What has actually happened to her?" Ashfaq shot the questions in one breath. Most Indians, across the entire subcontinent, irrespective of caste, creed and religion, address all the female nurses as 'Sister'.

"Please take a seat." The nurse pointed towards a metal chair placed across her working table and continued, "Your sister was brought here last night by some of her neighbours. She was bleeding profusely, I'm sure you can very well guess from where. After a thorough medical examination, the gynaecologist realised that the nearly fully-grown foetus had become absolutely still inside. So, in order to save your sister's life, the dead foetus was surgically removed immediately last night itself. Surprisingly, her husband was not seen anywhere around. So, on Zikra's request, we called you up."

"Hai Allah! But how did that happen?"

"Well, we are not certain. There was a cut on her lower abdomen probably caused by falling over a table corner or something like that. But your sister is not telling anything to us about how she got hurt. She is simply crying. As her husband is missing from the scene completely, we guess that most probably he is the root cause of all this. Anyway, please come back here around 12, at lunchtime. You can meet your sister. Please excuse me now." The nurse dismissed him.

Ashfaq freshened up and had a samosa and tea for breakfast. At 12 sharp he was there, outside the Female Ward. He was restless to meet Zikra.

"How are you my little sister? How did all this happen? Please tell me everything!" Ashfaq tenderly placed his hand on her forehead while speaking.

In reply Zikra looked up, clasped his hand with both her hands and started crying. Tears started rolling down his cheeks too. It was an emotional reunion of two distressed siblings.

"Bhai Jaan, I have been hiding a lot of things from you about my married life," Zikra spoke very slowly, with a lot of difficulty. "I had a blissful life the first year. But my in-laws started ill-treating me after I gave birth to Mehr. Typical of middle-class Indian mentality, they wanted a boy. When I started carrying the second baby, Barkat got after me to undergo the sex test. But somehow, I have been avoiding it so far. He was wild but somewhat under control. And then, yesterday morning I woke up with terrible pain in the stomach. I was running eighth month, you know Bhai Jaan. He quickly took me to a lady doctor's clinic nearby. She did an elaborate ultrasound test on me and gave some medicines. We came back home. After a while, as usual, he left for his office. But when he did not reach back home by six, his usual time, I got a little worried. So, I started calling him up. But he just did not take my calls. And when he finally reached back home quite late at night, he was badly drunk, stinking of alcohol. His eyes were red.

Poor little Mehr got mortally scared and hid behind me. From the doorstep itself he started shouting at me. From his highly slurred speech what I could make out was that while going to the office he had visited the clinic again; and after giving a generous bribe, found out from the doctor that I'm carrying another baby girl! That crazy husband of mine felt so disturbed that instead of going to the office, he straightaway headed for the local bar. Since then he had been drinking there, nonstop!" Zikra felt dryness in her throat so pointed her slender finger towards the water glass. Ashfaq very carefully lifted her head and poured water into her half-open mouth.

"As I was still feeling unwell, I didn't reply to his accusations and shouting. Instead, I served him dinner. He appeared quite hungry, because he finished his dinner very quickly. But he resumed screaming and abusing soon after. He asked me to abort the baby, again and again. When I reminded him that I'm eight months pregnant and aborting the child may cost my own life, he got terribly wild. For the first time ever since we got married, he started hitting me. I had been subjected to mental humiliation by him and his family members many times before but I was never beaten up earlier. I think the Satan in him had woken up from deep slumber. And you know what, all of a sudden he kicked my belly. I stumbled and fell with my face down. As I fell, my stomach, with my poor baby inside, hit the corner of our living room table. That's the last thing I remember before I fainted. I have lost my child Bhai Jaan!" She started sobbing uncontrollably.

Ashfaq's blood had reached boiling point by now. How could Barkat do such a horrible thing to Zikra! How could he kick her in the stomach! He was furious. He was not going to forgive his stupid, crazy-for-a-son brother-in-law for this. No! Never! He quickly got up from his seat, planted a light kiss on her forehead and left. Zikra got scared and started calling him, but he never looked back.

He hired an auto and reached his sister's house within fifteen minutes. The main door was open. He found little Mehr sitting in the living room holding her favourite teddy bear tightly and crying. It was one o'clock in the afternoon. He could hear that swine of a man Barkatullah snoring inside. He should have gone into the bedroom straightaway and banged his head on the wall. But right now, his heart bled for the poor girl. He sat down next to her and took the little child on his lap. In between sobs, with broken words, Mehr somehow managed to convey that she was given half a bottle of milk by her father in the morning, and that's all. Ashfaq went to the kitchen with Mehr in his lap and quickly prepared some cereal for her. She was so hungry that she started eating immediately on her own with her small little hands.

Leaving Mehr engrossed with her food in the kitchen, he now headed for the bedroom. Barkat was still snoring, though a little lightly. He banged open the door and screamed, "Barkat! You bloody pig! How dare you beat my sister! How dare you kick her?"

Barkat was jolted out of his sleep. He was still under the influence of the previous day's heavy intake of alcohol. Startled to see Ashfaq at home all of a sudden, he started to stammer, "Hey, what's the matter? When did you come? And where is…"

"Stop that nonsense! Zikra is in hospital fighting for

her life because of you! She lost her eight-month-old baby, thanks to you, once again! What kind of man are you? You bastard!" Ashfaq shouted at the top of his voice and dished out one solid punch. The punch landed right on half-dazed Barkat's nose. It started bleeding. Now Ashfaq went wild and started punching and kicking him all over. Within a few minutes Barkat was on the floor, bleeding profusely and panting for breath. As Ashfaq's onslaught was continuing unabated, Barkat started shouting, "Help… help… Please save me from this man. He is going to kill me. Someone please call the police quickly! Please help!" Hearing her father's cries, Mehr left her food halfway and started crying very loudly. Poor baby.

The commotion soon reached the neighbours. They gathered around the fighting duo. Some of them caught hold of Ashfaq and saved Barkat from further blows. They all knew the entire story of what had actually happened last night. So, none of them actually felt sympathetic towards Barkat. However, an elderly woman dialled 100 to call the police.

Ashfaq hugged and kissed little Mehr a number of times before getting into the police jeep. She would be looked after by a middle-aged woman living next door till Zikra recovered fully and came back home.

At the police station Ashfaq was put behind bars on charges of beating up his brother-in-law severely. A bleeding Barkatullah Khan himself had filed the FIR against him.

Ashfaq was in police custody for the very first time in his life. And he knew that being an outsider in this town, he would have to spend the night inside the lock up. Resigned to his fate for the time being, he settled down on the rickety cot placed inside the dingy cell.

Ashfaq did not repent his actions at all. In fact, he felt quite happy and contented instead. He had taught his erring brother-in-law a lesson, a lesson of his life! He loved his sister Zikra much more than himself. Since early childhood, he had always been protecting her. He recollected how he fought with two seniors in the school once after they had passed some lewd comments on her. He, single handed, broke one boy's right hand and the other's left leg. And much before that, he had saved Zikra, then an innocent child, from being hurt by his closest friend who turned out to be a rogue. He was very young then. At the lock up, he felt very hungry and sleepy at the same time. His tired and foggy mind slowly drifted back in time, to the early childhood days in his small, peaceful village....

"Ashfaq! Oye Ashfaq! Where are you?" Jamina Begum was shouting at the top of her voice. She continued to increase the pitch of her shrill voice while searching the whole house looking for her seven-year-old son.

"Oh here you are! Why are you hiding here, next to that heap of dung? Playing hide and seek with your friends, eh! There may be poisonous snakes inside. Come out, fast!" She was surprised to see Ashfaq trying to hide behind the mound of dried cow dung cakes at the far end of the house.

"Ya Allah! You are shivering so badly. You are running temperature too. Why are your eyes so very red? Where have you been? What the hell have you been doing exactly?" Jamina shot the volley of questions as she pulled him out of that dangerous spot. Snakes do frequent the cow dung mounds; they probably love coiling around those cakes and relish the smell too. Do snakes have a sense of smell? Allah only knows.

Ashfaq said nothing, just followed his Ammi to the kitchen. She made him sit on a small rectangular coir mat commonly found in the eastern part of the country. She pushed a white enamel coated plate towards him, filled with boiled rice, yellow lentil, a piece of fried fish and mixed vegetable curry. Ashfaq started eating lunch very quietly and slowly, with his trembling hands.

They lived in a small village named Kuchi Muchi on the outskirts of Chutia town, nearly 40 km east of Tezpur, Assam. Though Chutia is a rather small town but Tezpur has a population of more than a few lacs. But interestingly, being on the northern part of gigantic

Brahmaputra River, it is still not connected by rail properly. Their village is a typical one, found in scores all over the eastern part of India—be it Bengal, Assam or the plains of Arunachal Pradesh, dotted with small houses with a pond just behind. The size of the pond is generally dictated by the house owner's financial standing. A few bigger ponds are jointly owned by some close relatives too. In such cases, the relative's houses are generally built around the pond, thereby denying entry to outsiders completely. This ensures complete protection and safety of the entire progeny of marine life (fish, prawns and small crabs) flourishing inside the pond. And believe it or not, fish is the most prized possession of all rural Assamese and Bengalis alike. Where the ponds are jointly owned, fish breeding and fishing rights are given to one family at a time, generally for an entire year; though occasional big catches are shared with other families, merely as a goodwill gesture.

Jamina, for a minute or so, closely watched her otherwise soft-spoken son, now engrossed in savouring lunch; then she left the kitchen looking for her daughter, Zikra. With his mother gone, Ashfaq felt a bit more at ease. His hands became steady and the speed of swallowing food through the 'till now restrictive' throat picked up speed. After finishing lunch, he pushed the plate aside towards the big bucket of water for washing.

He was about to pick up the glass of water thoughtfully placed next to his plate by his mother when he suddenly heard a big commotion outside.

"Jamina, oh Jamina! Where is Ashfaq?" He could hear the distinctly melodious but definitely worried voice of Shabnam aunty. Jamina Begum appeared almost immediately from the pond side of their compact, small, independent house.

"Jamina Bi, there you are. Where is Ashfaq? I need to speak to him now, immediately." Shabnam sounded very edgy. Her husband Altaf appeared equally worried.

"Sure. But why are you looking so worried? What's the matter?" Jamina asked.

"Faraz is untraceable since morning. We have searched for him in the neighbourhood, asked everyone we have met so far but could not find him anywhere. I remember that your son Ashfaq and Faraz had gone out together in the morning to play. Where is Ashfaq? Is he back?" Shabnam spoke breathlessly.

Eight-year-old Faraz is the only child of Shabnam Begum and Altaf. They live about fifteen houses away. Faraz and Ashfaq are inseparable friends, almost since birth; everyone in Kuchi Muchi village knew that very well.

Before his mother could call out his name, Ashfaq appeared from the kitchen. He was quite steady and by now his hands had stopped shaking completely. He reached the centre of the courtyard and spoke, "Salaam Alaikum Khala! What happened?" He always addressed Shabnam aunty as Khala, though they were not related.

"Where is my Faraz? I saw you both heading towards the Maidan in the morning. So where has he gone? We have been looking for him everywhere. Tell me quickly, when did you get back home? And where is he?"

Ashfaq shuffled his feet, clasped his arms over his chest, took a deep breath and started to reply, "Khala, you are right. We both had gone to the village ground to play in the morning. Other boys also joined us there and we started playing hide and seek around the trees and bushes. But after a while it became unbearably hot and humid. So, all of us decided to stop playing and go back home. But Faraz wanted to go fishing and asked me to accompany him. I always go with him everywhere, that you know. But today, because of the deadly sun I just refused to go with him to the pond in your backyard. That's why I came back home nearly two hours ago, you can ask Ammi jaan. Have you checked the pond?"

"Checked the pond? No, we've looked for him around the pond. Allah, have mercy on us! Let's go and search the pond side once more. I'm sure Faraz is hiding somewhere, just to tease us. He is safe, inshallah!" Shabnam started running towards her house. Altaf, Jamina and Ashfaq followed her.

All four of them searched for Faraz around the pond once again but in vain.

"Altaf Bhai, why don't you search the pond itself? Just to rule out, I mean." Jamina suggested hesitantly.

"What the hell? How can you even think of such a..." Shabnam started shouting at Jamina. But before she could finish, Altaf raised his right hand indicating his wife to stop. He then looked up probably seeking divine intervention from above and jumped into the pond.

"Here Uncle, search this side." Ashfaq pointed towards a particular spot inside the pond which also happened to be the deepest end. At once Altaf, Shabnam and Jamina gave him surprised, questioning looks.

Ashfaq gave a sad smile in return. "This is the exact spot where he generally stands and throws the bait while fishing. That's why I suggested it," he sheepishly said.

Without wasting any more time, Altaf dived in the location pointed out by Ashfaq. All others waited on the edge of the pond anxiously. It was an eternal wait.

'Whoosh....' Suddenly Altaf popped up from the water with a lot of force. And there was Faraz on his shoulder, his hands and legs dangling loosely! Shabnam screamed at the top of her voice. Jamina too started howling. And Ashfaq froze!

Faraz was wearing black shorts and a chequered multi-coloured half-sleeve shirt, with no undergarments.

In villages, boys under ten generally avoid wearing undergarments, even to the schools. The girls, too, generally don't start using a bra until some of their assets become fairly big and literally eye-catching!

Altaf, with Faraz on his shoulder, reached them as fast as he could. He very gently lowered Faraz down on the ground and tried to revive him, pressing his chest vigorously and giving mouth to mouth resuscitation. But alas, nothing worked. It appeared to be a hopeless case of drowning! The womenfolk were crying louder than before. Hearing such a hue and cry, all the neighbours also gathered around.

Probably as a last-ditch attempt, Altaf suddenly picked up the still body of his beloved son and held him over his head with both hands, and then he started revolving around himself. Anger, helplessness and sheer desperation made his face stone-hard and his eyes blood red. His unusual moves resembled the 'Tandav-Nritya', the terrifying dance of Lord Shiva with the mortal remains of his beloved wife Sati! Ashfaq felt terribly scared looking at his friend's dad. He closed his eyes and started praying for his dearest friend, trembling. Suddenly something fell on Ashfaq's feet. He quickly opened his eyes to see what it was. It was a small lump of shit which had escaped Faraz's shorts and landed directly on Ashfaq's feet! Maybe while drowning, out of horrific fear, Faraz had passed the stool. And now the dangling body going around in circles over his father's head had made the lump escape. Was it just a coincidence? Or was it a stern message from Allah? Everyone gathered around the scene and stared at Ashfaq. The little boy shivered inside.

After a while Altaf also gave up. He delicately lowered Faraz's body on to the ground. By then the village doctor had also arrived at the scene; some concerned neighbour had called him. The old doctor kneeled down next to Faraz and picked up his right hand to examine it. All eyes were fixated on him now. After two minutes he let go Faraz's hand and shook his head. It was a silent confirmation of the most bitter truth of life—Death!

From the circumstances, it was presumed by all that while fishing with the rod, somehow, he must have lost balance and slipped into the pond and drowned. Being only eight years old, Faraz did not know how to swim. How sad!

All hell broke loose immediately. Shabnam and all other women gathered around were somehow holding themselves up till now. Suddenly their loud, uncontrollable cries filled the air, echoing around pathetically. It was terribly heart-wrenching! The wailing made all the men present cry in silence, except probably the sixty-plus experienced doctor, who had seen enough of life and death; therefore, he remained unmoved.

A speechless Ashfaq sat down next to Faraz. Very slowly he picked up both his limp, lifeless hands and kept staring at the slightly swollen-up face of his best friend. Tears started rolling down his cheeks wetting the ground underneath. His little sister Zikra had reached the pond by then. She was now standing nearby looking at Faraz and sobbing.

Faraz was buried a few hours later inside the village cemetery. Shabnam and Altaf were absolutely inconsolable. They had lost their only child! That too in such a horrible way and at such a tender age!

It was one o'clock in the night. Ashfaq was wide awake in his small bed. He was just not getting sleep. What had actually happened in the morning kept coming back to him again and again. His mind went back to what had happened the previous day….

...Yesterday, in the sunny summer afternoon, after finishing lunch, Ashfaq leisurely strolled across to Faraz's house with the intention of playing Ludo, a very popular indoor game in India, with his best friend. As expected, Shabnam Khala and her husband had gone off to the field to supervise the labourers. So, he knew Faraz would be alone at home. Thinking of bringing in an element of surprise, he tiptoed towards Faraz's bedroom. But Faraz was not alone. He could hear giggling sounds inside. It was definitely a girl, a very young girl. Who could it be?

Curious, Ashfaq decided not to bang open the bedroom door. He slowly went to the side window, parted the lace curtain slightly and peeped inside.

Hai Allah! His dear sister Zikra was lying on the bed with her frock removed and thrown aside. She was wearing only a small pink panty and Faraz was sitting on the bed with a plastic toy stethoscope in his hand examining Zikra. They were playing 'Doctor-Doctor'!

Furious but curious at the same time, Ashfaq decided to see it all. So, he continued to peep inside. Aping an experienced doctor, Faraz plugged the stethoscope into his ears and placed the sensor on Zikra's chest. The little girl felt amused and giggled. He then slowly moved it down and placed it over her naval. She felt tickled and giggled again, a little louder this time. Probably encouraged by her response, Faraz became bold. "Hmm...I will have to examine you further, more deeply. So patient Zikra please undress quickly. Please remove your panty now," a serious Dr Faraz ordered his little patient.

"No Doctor please!" The five-year-old patient pleaded feebly; she probably felt ashamed.

"Nothing doing! You know the rules of this game. You must obey the doctor fully, then only I can examine you properly and tell you about your condition. So, do exactly what I say. When you play the role of the doctor after this, and I become your patient, I will do whatever you ask me to. I promise!" Dr Faraz was adamant. So, very sheepishly, Zikra removed her pink cotton panty, kept it aside and got ready for further examination.

Standing still outside the window, Ashfaq was watching everything. He was boiling inside by now, but somehow made up his mind to see the entire proceedings, come what may. He must know where it ended finally.

"All right. That's like a good patient. Now lie still," Faraz ordered her. He then very playfully placed the stethoscope in between her thighs. She felt quite funny and ticklish. Though just five years old, somehow, she felt a little embarrassed too. So, she did not giggle this time, just kept quiet. And she innocently kept staring at her doctor, probably trying to guess his next move.

"Okay Zikra, now let me check the temperature inside your body. It is very important, you see," Faraz said in a serious doctorly tone. He then gently raised both her legs. Then he kept the stethoscope aside and took out a small thermometer from the Doctor-kit. Faraz shook the plastic thermometer a number of times like an experienced professional, looked at the unsuspecting Zikra, grinned playfully and suddenly inserted it inside her!

"Oh no! It is hurting! Take it out now," Zikra screamed, doling out an instinctive kick to his violating hand and sat up on the bed crying. Faraz was taken aback.

That was enough! Ashfaq went nearly mad. He just banged the wooden window hard and ran out of Faraz's house in complete disgust, fuming with anger.

"Oh hell, who is there? Come on, speak up!" A visibly panicked Faraz came out of the bedroom, running. But there was no one to be seen. A terribly angry Ashfaq had vanished into the shrubs nearby.

Ashfaq continued running like a mad bull on a rampage till he reached the far end of their village. He sat under the big Banyan tree next to the village playground, all alone. He was very, very angry with Faraz, his bosom friend for years. How could he do such terrible things to Zikra, his cute little sister? He felt like going back and bashing up Faraz right now, inside his own house. But Ashfaq knew it well that being younger and lighter than Faraz, he himself would get bashed up instead. So, he thought of a plan—a sinister plan in his small but furious mind. He must save his little innocent sister from such horrible things, and from such horrible guys, at any cost. Faraz was no longer his friend. Inside his small but cunning brain, he modified and remodified his plan a number of times till it reached perfection. Happy, he left for home at sunset as there are no street lights in his village. Venturing out after sunset without a torch is quite dangerous, thanks to the poisonous snakes, scorpions and the plentiful blood-hungry leeches.

He found his darling little sister at home enjoying evening tea and rusks. She appeared a little tense. But she was not crying anymore. Nor was she complaining to her mother about any pain. Maybe she hasn't got hurt that badly. Probably her instinctive reaction of kicking Faraz and Ashfaq's window-banging had saved her. Anyway, Faraz had to pay....

This morning, as per the plan, he finished his breakfast and left for Faraz's house as if nothing had happened. From there both of them went to the playground and along with a handful others played hide and seek. After a while, when the others left, it was Ashfaq himself and not Faraz, who suggested that they both should go fishing in the pond behind Faraz's house. Ashfaq deliberately chose Faraz's pond because he knew that Jamina, his own mother, would be in and around their own house and the pond, either washing utensils or tending to the cows. Whereas Faraz's father was definitely in his shop in the morning and Shabnam Khala in the fields to supervise the tilling, as usual.

After reaching home, Faraz took out his locally improvised fishing kit and headed for the pond, with Ashfaq following him. He went towards the deepest end as chances of catching fish were definitely the best there. He dug out an earthworm, used it as the bait and threw the hook into the water with maximum force. Ashfaq stood behind him, watching the proceedings intently. As Faraz settled down with his apparatus, Ashfaq started without any warning, "So, you found only my innocent little sister to play 'Doctor-Doctor' with? How shameful of you!"

Faraz was completely taken aback. Badly shaken up, he meekly asked, "How do you know? Was that you at the window?"

An agitated Ashfaq retorted, "Yes, that was me watching you hurting my poor sister! How could you betray my trust so badly you stupid fellow!"

By now Faraz had somehow regained some of his composure and inborn smartness. He smiled and replied, "If you really feel so hurt, I'm sorry. But you know what, if you wish, you too can play doctor-doctor with my sister."

Ashfaq just did not appreciate the reply. He quipped, "Don't act oversmart. You don't have a sister; we both know that very well!"

"Okay, don't be so upset with me. With passage of time, if your little sister Zikra grows up to become a beautiful woman, well, one day I might marry her, you never know. And then, from being a friend, you will become my brother-in-law. And then I can call you, 'Oye Saala, come here'! Ha…Ha…Ha…" Faraz laughed out loudly appreciating his own stupid joke.

It was too much for Ashfaq to tolerate. "You bloody pig! How dare you?" He screamed and pushed Faraz from behind with all his might. It was so sudden that Faraz just didn't get any time to react or to hold his ground. He tumbled down into the deepest part of the pond, still holding the fishing rod tightly.

Ashfaq stood still and watched his good friend Faraz trying to come out of the water a couple of times, gasping for breath and going down soon after. The desperate left hand of a dying Faraz resurfaced one last time before vanishing inside the pond for good. Ashfaq sped back home, like a deer chased by a leopard, and hid himself behind the mound of cow dung cakes. Faraz would not play doctor-doctor with his innocent little sister Zikra and hurt her any more. Never!

At the tender age of seven, Ashfaq had killed a human being, his best friend! A cold-blooded murder! But he was not repenting at all. He just felt scared! Scared of getting caught.

Maybe that lump of shit falling on his feet was indeed a stern warning from almighty Allah!

Time and tide wait for none. After about six months, Shabnam conceived for the second time. And nine months later, a beautiful baby girl was born in their house. Very surprisingly, she had a birthmark, a small, oval shaped black patch on the right side of her lower back, just below the rib cage, exactly the same location where Faraz had one. This unusual coincidence made everyone in remote Kuchi Muchi village believe that Faraz had taken rebirth in the same household, as a lovely girl child this time. Delighted, Altaf and Shabnam named the newborn daughter, their new-found bundle of joy after their son Faraz as 'Farzana'.

As prevalent in most Indian villages, Farzana was born at home, duly aided by 'Daima', the grand old village midwife. And being very close family friends, Ashfaq, Zikra and their parents visited Shabnam and Altaf the same evening. Ashfaq was nearly nine years old then. Newborn Farzana looked so small, so cute and so very innocent. Something urged him to like her instantly. Was it her cuteness? Or her innocence? Or the acute guilt feeling in his little demonic heart? He was not sure. But whatever, he had fallen in love with Farzana the day she was born. And from that very day, Ashfaq has always been around Farzana like a shadow, watching her grow—from a little toddler to an 18-year-old fully developed, beautiful woman, laughing with her and shielding her from all possible ills. Like all other villagers of Kuchi Muchi, did he too see a glimpse of his deceased (murdered) friend Faraz in her? Allah only knows!

Ashfaq loves Farzana a lot. And he knows that Farzana loves him too. Since her early childhood, he has been her constant companion, brother (no way!), friend, philosopher and guide. She knew only one man in her life. Whenever she encountered any problem, any difficulty in her life, without batting an eyelid she instantly fell back on Ashfaq.

After completing graduation, Ashfaq picked up a private job and started doing fairly well for himself. His sister Zikra was also married off into a reasonably good household. So, when Farzana turned eighteen, Ashfaq cornered his mother one fine day and expressed his desire to marry her. On Ashfaq's insistence, two months ago, Jamina Begum quite hesitantly approached Shabnam and Altaf for the alliance. To their utter surprise, it was almost instantly accepted! So, in another month's time, he is slated to read the sacred, the most awaited Nikahnama with his beloved Farzana!

Inside the small lockup, Ashfaq smiled to himself, a wicked, joyous, playful but satisfying smile. Just one month later, after getting married, he was going to play Doctor-Doctor with beautiful Farzana, day in, day out!

Allah is great! He has always been great and forgiving! Especially with him!

The Bangkok Fiasco

"Good morning Sunil sir! Heartiest congratulations! Our children have successfully completed first six months of their marriage," Captain Amodh Kumar Tiwari of the Indian Navy proudly spoke to Mr Sunil Popli, father of Sushil, his recently acquired son-in-law.

Sunil was equally elated. In today's fast-forward life, stability in marriage is really very important. At least that is what more than half-a-century old people like Sunil, Amodh and their respective wives think.

"A very good morning and congratulations to all of you too! Payal is a very mature girl and so is our Sushil. I'm sure they both will sail through this journey of life together very smoothly." Sunil sounded very optimistic.

For retired Captain Amodh Kumar Tiwari, 'AKT' of the Indian Navy, any mention of water, ship or sailing made his adrenalin glands secrete extra juices instantly. Plus, Sunil's rather positive observation on his daughter's level of maturity made him happy. 'How's the josh?' 'High sir.' So with a lot of josh, he replied, "Yes, you are right. They both make a perfect couple. So what's the plan for the evening? Let's all meet up somewhere and celebrate. How about the club?"

"Well, frankly speaking we have not planned anything to celebrate their six months of togetherness. Being a normal weekday, Sujata and I will have to go to office as usual. But we both can always manage things in the office and reach the club by eight pm. What about Payal and Sushil? Honestly, I am yet to call them up to even wish them."

"Okay, we will finalise our plan well before lunchtime. I haven't congratulated them so far either. Let me call up. So, see you both in the evening." Amodh hung up on Sunil and almost immediately dialled his beloved daughter's mobile number.

"Hello Papa!" The standard phrase greeted him from the other end. Irrespective of the place, situation, mood, country (Switzerland, while on honeymoon, for example) and time of day, Payal always started her conversation with her dear dad with the same phrase. It always sounded like soothing music to his ears! Payal has a nice, soft, melodious voice.

"Good morning Mota Bhai! Our heartiest congrats to you and dear Sushil. And you know for what, isn't it?" Amodh sounded very happy. Payal had been a healthy child all through, but she was always trying her level best to reduce the circumference of her tummy and total body weight. Since she could not stay away from good food for more than three to four hours at a stretch, she never succeeded in achieving what she wished. But just about a year ago, before her marriage, she became very serious about slimming down. So, she urged her ever-willing Dad to procure a treadmill. However, rigorous exercises on the treadmill and her subsequent four-hourly super-meals continued side by side. As a result, she neither reduced nor gained any weight after one year, at the time of her big, fat wedding.

Luckily, the treadmill was brought home on short-term lease. So, soon after her marriage Amodh sent back the cumbersome and useless (for him and his family) apparatus to its owner company.

A few days after their wedding, Payal and Sushil moved out to a small but tastefully done up flat in Gurugram. With a whole lot of relatives and friends in and around Delhi, they continued to attend birthday parties, engagements, weddings and social events very frequently. So, for Payal's weight, there was no looking back now. She kept putting on weight, though slowly, gram by gram. On the other hand, being a tough-nut naval officer, Capt Amodh always maintained himself. So, when all hopes of Payal slimming down became a distant dream for him and the family, he jokingly started calling his beloved daughter 'Mota Bhai'. In Gujarati it actually means elder brother and not fat brother. But the doting father liked the adjective and his 'always happy' daughter didn't mind it either.

"Thank you, Papa. Yes, I do know the reason. We both will be leaving for office shortly. No plans so far, but we can always meet up in the evening somewhere to celebrate."

"Well, in that case reach the club by 7.30 pm sharp. Your in-laws have promised to be there by eight. Okay, don't be late," diehard naval officer passed his order and hung up.

Most of us civilians are confused about the complicated rank structure of our elite defence forces. Captain of army and navy appear to be the same. And why not! Well, this is a sore point, especially for the naval officers. An Army Captain is a junior officer whereas a Naval Captain is a fairly senior officer, equivalent to a Colonel of the Army and a Group Captain of the Air Force! So, in order to make the common man understand the difference, majority of Naval Captains prefer to suffix their rank with IN, i.e. Indian Navy. So, they actually write 'Captain (IN)'. Unfortunately, a large number of

Indians still read that as Captain (In), as in Doctor (In) / Doctor (Out) boards found hanging outside the doctor's clinic! This is a sad fact and not a silly joke, believe me!

That evening, the Tiwaris and the Poplis met at the club for a small family get together. Mrs Manju Tiwari and Mrs Sujata Popli soon got engrossed in discussing the most serious issue, 'the maid's problem', holding Mojitos (European nimbupani wherein pudina leaves float around in a loose, characterless manner). On the next sofa, Sushil, Payal and her younger brother Anuj started voicing their individual opinions on various technicalities of the latest mobiles available in the market. While sipping his second drink of the evening, Amodh generally looked at everybody and asked, "So, my dear Sushil, have you and your beloved wife chalked out any plans to celebrate your first wedding anniversary? You went to Switzerland for your honeymoon; so you should go out this time too. What do you say, Sunil sir? Am I making sense or not!"

Though only two drinks down, Sunil appeared quite high-spirited. "Why only them? Why don't we all like tonight make that a family outing? Let's go to some foreign country nearby," he immediately replied. Surprisingly, his instantaneous proposal was soon seconded by both the ladies.

As Sushil had come directly from his office, he was

carrying the office laptop. So he, Payal and Anuj, the tech-savvy trio, soon started browsing for a suitable family getaway. After about fifteen minutes of searching, they zeroed in on Thailand as the most *Sastaa-Tikao* (value-for-money) destination. All of them gave a thumbs up for it almost immediately and unanimously. So, it was decided that one day prior to the young couple's wedding anniversary, they all would land up in Phuket. After three nights there, both the families would fly out to Bangkok, the capital city, for two more nights. The serious discussion on flights and hotel bookings was soon adjourned sine-die as aroma of sizzling hot snacks penetrated their nostrils.

Though the itinerary was carefully chosen and tickets and hotel room bookings were done well in advance, things were not working out as desired. Just two weeks before departure, Anuj expressed his inability to be part of the entourage as he failed to get leave from his new boss, who had joined his office just about a month back. So, his tickets and other bookings were cancelled, at a loss, of course. But the families were in for a rude shock when, with only three days left for departure, Sunil had to suddenly pull out as his boss wanted him to visit the company headquarters in Dubai for some very urgent work. Job takes priority over leisure, always and everywhere. Man proposes, Boss disposes!

So, on the day of the journey five reluctant souls, namely Captain (IN) AK Tiwari (Retd), Mrs Manju Tiwari, Sushil, Payal and Mrs Sujata Popli headed for the IGI Airport, Terminal 3. Manju was unhappy because her dear son Anuj was not on board. Sujata was very unhappy because she had made some secret plans to enjoy this trip, with her husband in tow of course. But unfortunately, he was not coming. Their moods remained subdued throughout the flight to Phuket, but somehow became alright, rather joyous during the subsequent road journey from the airport to the hotel. At the hotel, Amodh and Manju and Sushil and Payal checked into a double bedroom each. Lonely, poor Sujata took up an adjacent single room. Tired, they all had an early dinner and retired for the night.

Amodh was up and awake at 7 am the next morning. He prepared bed tea and relished it before going for a bath. After doing his puja, he woke up Manju who was a late riser since childhood and a little unwell since yesterday. By nine, Amodh had hit the streets of Phuket looking for a cake shop to buy a nice cake for the young couple. Surprisingly, there were hardly any bakeries nearby. Finally, after an hour-long search and relentless inquiring about it, he managed to get an ice cream cake from a famous local outlet.

The cake was cut by the couple a little after breakfast. Both Sunil from far away Dubai and Anuj from Delhi marked their presence through video calling, a modern-day technical wonder. Then they all set course on foot for the beach. The main beach of Phuket is well maintained and appeared neat and clean. It becomes a lively, attractive joint after sunset when numerous restaurants across the road open their extension counters very close to the waterline. After spending considerable time at the beach, they felt hungry and headed for what appeared to be an Indian restaurant to savour seafood.

"Hello! Namaste! Sat Sri Akaal! *Tusi Indian ho*? Welcome, welcome!" The manager bent forward while greeting them. Floored by his Punjabi, they all walked in and settled down in comfortable chairs. A Lassi jug, glasses and menu card appeared soon after.

Sujata did not like seafood as such, except fish, that too occasionally. She always looked at prawns with suspicion and considered them as creepy creatures. So, a chicken dish was ordered for her. The restaurant otherwise served jumbo prawns, squids, crabs, lobster and a host of other lesser known seafoods. Captain Tiwari, an experienced seafarer who had visited most of the seaports around the world, decided to order squids, jumbo prawns, fish and masala crabs for the remaining four people. As the menu card quoted the price for 100 grams of each and the rate looked quite steep, he ordered 100 grams of each dish. The manager kept them engaged with small talk about India and Delhi for next half an hour till the food arrived on the table. It was a real shocker! The waiter filled up the entire big table with five plates of 100 grams of each type of dish ordered—chicken, fish, squid, jumbo prawns and crabs! Amodh gave a surprised, agitated look to the humble looking manager. He, in return, politely reminded Amodh that he had ordered 100 grams of each dish. So, they had prepared 100 grams for each one of them, that is a neat half a kg of chicken, fish, squid, crabs and jumbo prawns, each!

It is considered prudent to always order a little extra food because, while treating yourself lavishly, especially in a foreign land, food should not fall short. If required it can be carried to the hotel for consumption later. But what these people had done was utter nonsense! By then, with his past experiences of meeting people across the globe, Captain Amodh had realised that the manager and the staff were actually not Indians! They were, in fact, Lahori Pakis! It soon became crystal clear to him that the Pakis, at least once, had managed to make Charlies out of the Indians!

He sighed and asked everybody to attack the food at once! Feeling cornered, they all ate to their heart's content.

But still a huge quantity of food was left. So Payal asked the waiter to pack the unconsumed food. And then came the bill. Lo and behold! It was a whopping Rs 13,700, in Baht of course!

'Bloody bastard,' Amodh murmured while clearing the bill. Though born in the interiors of Bihar, he had done his schooling from Military School Chail, situated in the Himalayas, and then joined the prestigious National Defence Academy, Khadakwasla, Pune. So he actually had an unlimited vocabulary of choicest abuse words. Feeling cheated, he deliberately did not give any tip to the waiter.

Anyhow, undeterred and wishing to continue with the celebrations, they went for dinner to a beach-side restaurant which specialised in Thai cuisine. Unlike the afternoon, here the music, cocktails and local food were really good. Soon all five of them forgot about the bitter experience of the afternoon and started enjoying.

Payal was holding a glass of Screwdriver in her hand and was busy enjoying the soulful music played by the live band. "Excuse me, Ma'am!" She got a little startled suddenly hearing a man's voice just behind her. She quickly turned her head. It was the same man who had been serving them drinks and snacks for the last half an hour or so. "You are Payal Ma'am, right? I am Montu Kipgen, remember? I had joined the hotel as a waiter and you were the Assistant Manager. When you first walked in here, I recognised you immediately, but was not 100 per cent sure. Now I just heard this gentleman sitting next to you calling your name. Do you recollect me now, Ma'am?" The short, fair young man appeared to urge her to recognise him.

Payal's multi-skilled brain was immediately redirected to her own office file! She was the Assistant Manager in the HR dept of a five-star hotel chain. She now remembered this cute young lad from Manipur. After doing his graduation he had come to Delhi looking for a suitable job in order to sustain himself and his poor family. But in Delhi, who gives a good job to just a graduate? That too from a normal, 'nothing to write home about' college! Frustrated after a series of rejections, he had finally joined their hotel chain as a waiter about two years ago. Being from a small town, he was very honest, dependable, sincere and dedicated to his profession and to his customers too.

Payal also remembered that during the unfortunate terrorist attacks on the innocent guests of Mumbai's Taj Mahal Palace Hotel on 26/11, the hotel staff chose not to run away. In fact, most of them had literally staked their own lives to save the guests. In the process, a few of them had made the supreme sacrifice too. A case-study was later conducted in a very reputed management institute abroad on the subject, to analyse the psyche of the staff who went well beyond their call of duty. To everyone's surprise, it was revealed that most of them belonged to lower middle-class families from small towns and villages across the country, born and brought up with basic family values and ethics. That's why they chose to risk their own lives for the guests. 'Atithi Devo Bhava' in true sense!

Montu was no exception. He served well and smilingly. But unfortunately, after spending just about six months on the job, for some inexplicable reason, one fine morning he just e-mailed his resignation to her and left. In fact, she called him up in order to make him reconsider his decision but it was of no use.

Payal felt happy to see him again, but at the same time she felt sad to see him working as a waiter here. "Hello Montu! So nice to see you again, that too in such a faraway place. This is Sushil, my husband. We got married last year. So, how's life here?" Payal ended her reply with a question.

"Oh, fine ma'am. Good to know that you have recognised me." Montu felt elated. He had a lot of regard for Payal Madam. She was known for her uprightness, fairness in dealing with everyone and above all, for her kind-heartedness. In fact, he wanted to get her some discount tonight. But the restaurant rules didn't permit such things for tourists Alas!

"Montu, when you mailed your resignation to me, I

had asked you the reason for leaving such a reputed hotel chain as ours, that too so soon. But you never replied. That's of course completely your choice, so it's fine with me. But please tell me, if you had to continue doing the same job, then why did you leave a five-star hotel chain in your own country and choose a small restaurant in a faraway foreign land instead? I really find that quite intriguing."

"Ma'am, you want to know why I left the hotel and also India? Well, I left because from the very first day I was called a 'Chinky' inside the hotel by so-called colleagues of mine, as well as outside on the streets by the unknown passers-by and also by my neighbours. I was constantly reminded that I was actually an outsider in my own country. I felt highly offended and fed up! And that's why I left the hotel as well as the country. And here I am! No one insults me here, believe me! I do this job only in the evening, during the rush hours. I get paid enough to sustain my family. And there is dignity of labour here, Ma'am! You very well know what the social standing of a waiter in India is. And further, to progress in life, I am also doing an MBA through correspondence, hoping to complete by next year-end. You know Madam, it is far better to be accepted as an outsider in a foreign country than to be treated like one in your own country! I mean it, I really do!" Montu looked extremely angry and hurt.

Not only Payal but all five of them were intently listening to Montu's story. There prevailed a pin drop silence, occasionally broken by the sounds of waves hitting the shoreline, probably with similar anger and frustration!

Montu's last sentence was rather hard-hitting. But at the same time, it was the truth, a very bitter truth! A big black blot on our so-called educated, cultured society! People in India don't waste a nano-second to call people names, or to insult somebody. The docile, friendly folks from the North Eastern states are constantly humiliated and harassed. When will we change? Change for good! God only knows.

Captain Amodh got up instantly and hugged Montu. It was a warm and friendly hug. He was soon followed by Sushil. A little while later Payal stood up and took Montu's hand for a warm shake, "I'm sorry Montu. I wish you had told me this. I would have taken those third-rate idiots to task, even thrown them out! You know it's better to have an empty stable than mad horses in it!"

Montu felt flabbergasted. Had he spoken too much, too soon? He nervously nodded his head and went off to fetch the next round of drinks for his valued Indian guests.

After dinner while leaving the restaurant, Payal called Montu aside. She pushed a bundle of Thai currency notes into his reluctant palm. "Montu I know you are badly hurt by the behaviour of some of your, I mean, our own country-cousins. But any time you decide to return to India, and to Delhi in particular, just send me an e-mail. Though it is against our company policy to re-engage someone who has resigned his job earlier, I will go all out to make a special case for you. I would love to see your innocent, smiling face in the lobby of our famous hotel once again. And if you wish, I can also get you transferred to our hotel in Guwahati. I'm sure no one will call you names there. Take care, Montu," Payal left the restaurant with a heavy heart and moist eyes.

The next morning, the group minus Manju left for sightseeing after breakfast. Manju was not keeping well since they took off from Delhi itself. She had been suffering from stomach-ache, nausea and respiratory problems. Due to all these, she couldn't sleep properly the previous night. So, the problems had worsened further. She refused to have breakfast in the morning. Amodh decided to stay back to look after his beloved wife but she vehemently negated that too.

"All of us have come here to enjoy. So what if I'm a little sick! Life must go on. I'm old but capable enough to look after myself. From seven we have come down to just five! So, let's not go for any more compromises and sacrifices to reduce it further. Please just carry on; see you all in the evening." Manju spoke in a very straightforward manner. Amodh was, therefore, left with no choice but to proceed for the planned, prepaid bus tour.

In the bus Sushil and Payal promptly occupied two adjacent seats at the rear. Well, they were a honeymoon couple, they deserved some privacy! So, Amodh and Sujata had to occupy seats in the front row and perforce had to sit next to each other. It was almost a daylong tour so soon they got talking to each other. Sujata was upset because she had been touring without her husband. Amodh was upset because he was unaccompanied by his ailing wife. So, they both decided to cheer each other up.

"Sujata ji, you look very upset. All of us know the reason behind it. It was an unavoidable circumstance due to which Sunil had to miss this holiday. So, I request you to please cheer up and enjoy the trip. I'm sure your hubby will not like to hear that his wife roamed around entire Thailand with a grumpy face!"

"I think you are right Amodh ji. Let's forget about what has happened and enjoy the present. I also request that you forget about Manju's sickness and cheer up."

In reply Amodh took out two cans of chilled coke from his small backpack, offered her one and loudly said, "Cheers!" This made Sujata laugh out freely for the very first time since leaving Delhi. The ice was broken.

Over next one hour they sipped coke occasionally

and spoke with each other on subjects ranging from Discovery Channel's programmes to rising petrol prices to the prevailing Venezuelan crisis. Captain Amodh, being from the navy, had travelled the world so, he was very knowledgeable on various subjects and could articulate well. Sujata, on the other hand, was a typical happy-go-lucky government servant who felt elated while receiving the three per cent annual increment in July every year; she also felt overjoyed once every tenth year with the announcement of the Central Pay Commission! She, expectedly, did not have much worldly knowledge beyond the birds and the bees, and the scarcity of maids in Delhi. She, therefore, got thoroughly impressed with her son's father-in-law. For Amodh, an avid talker, Sujata turned out to be a good listener.

They finally returned to the hotel at dinner time. It was an enjoyable outing for all four of them. Manju had had a light lunch and was comfortable in her room. They shared their day's experiences with her turn by turn, making her feel very important. And why not! Poor thing had missed all the fun!

With an entire day's rest, Manju felt much better next morning. So, after breakfast at the hotel they all went out for a leisurely stroll. Like one finds paan shops in UP and Bihar in every nook and corner of a street, here in Phuket and Bangkok the massage parlours are found in abundance.

"Helloo Madaam... Massage Please..." The highly nasal but melodious pleading of the local women kept on greeting them through the entire busy street. As there was no fixed agenda for the morning, Sujata and Manju abruptly stopped near one such parlour. "Let's all go for body massage here so that after going back to India we can proudly tell everyone that we have taken a Thai massage. What do you say, Manju?" Sujata appeared to look for some moral support.

"Yes, of course. Let's talk to the manager," Manju quickly replied. She had missed out on the previous day's tour, thus was very keen to go ahead with some activity.

The remaining three quietly followed the ladies towards the manager's counter. "We are three women and two men. Do you have men masseurs here to give body massage to these two?" Sujata inquired in proper English. The manager-cum-owner gave her a blank look. She had not understood anything.

Captain Amodh had been to a few of the ports in this far eastern part of Asia before. So, he immediately understood the problem and took over from Sujata. "He and I (pointing at Sushil) want massage by men (he showed his well-kept moustache to indicate a man) only. You have men?" Amodh took some time to put across their requirement.

"Oh, no, no, no! In Thailand only we massage (she

indicated all the women standing near her). No boys here. We give good massage. Very cheap. I give you good discount," she replied in broken English.

Manju and Sujata exchanged glances before agreeing to her proposal. "All right. These two women will take them, okay." Manju picked out two elderly women for Amodh and Sushil.

So, very reluctantly and unwillingly, for next one hour both the men got massaged by two senior citizens of Thailand! "So, how was it? Enjoyed?" Payal jokingly asked Sushil. In reply she received a dirty look from her hubby. She quickly walked away from him.

As per the schedule, next day they caught the morning flight to Bangkok and reached the pre-booked 3-star hotel by lunch time. Manju was feeling quite uneasy throughout the two-hour flight. She had visited the Departure Lounge toilet just before boarding the flight. But still she used the aeroplane toilet thrice in two hours. This phenomenon of frequent urination worried her husband. She looked very tired and pale too. So Amodh ordered lunch for everyone in his room. Manju had very little of it and dozed off to sleep within no time. Actually, all of them had woken up very early to catch the 6.30 am flight. Tired, all of them went off to their respective rooms for a well-deserved afternoon siesta.

Amodh woke up around 6 pm. As Manju was unwell

and still sleeping, he decided to boil two cups of water and make tea for both of them before waking her up. But surprisingly, when he called her five minutes later, Manju just did not respond. He shook her gently but still no reply! Scared, he immediately called out for Payal, Sushil and Sujata. They all tried to wake her up, but she appeared to be in semi-comatose state. While trying to shake her from deep sleep, Sujata realised that Manju's bed was wet. She had unknowingly passed urine in her sleep, thus her side of the giant bed was soiled. Terribly alarmed, Sushil quickly called up the Desk Manager on Intercom and explained the problem. The on-duty hotel doctor arrived after about ten minutes. After a quick preliminary examination, he suggested that she be taken to a hospital without wasting any time. Left with no other option, Amodh took the help of the doctor to ask for an ambulance and took Manju to the Emergency Ward of a reputed hospital nearby.

Thanks to modern-day online travel insurance policies, she was admitted as an indoor patient almost immediately. And it was a cashless admission.

"Well, I've asked for a number of tests to be done on the patient. As of now, it's a suspected case of UTI, (Urinary Tract Infection). And it is an acute one at that! But that can be confirmed only by tomorrow morning, after we have all the test reports. By the way, was she having the most visible symptom of frequent urination for a while? How come you people did not realise and put an adult diaper on her!" The doctor on duty had come out to question them. He looked fairly surprised at their ignorance.

"Sorry doctor! We are tourists from India; we landed in Thailand about four days back. For the last two days she had been complaining of some kind of general uneasiness but never told me anything about her bladder problem. Yesterday we all had gone out on a sightseeing tour of Phuket for the whole day but she refused to go with us. So, I really don't know how many times she visited the toilet yesterday. But yes, today, while travelling from Phuket to Bangkok, she did use the aeroplane toilet a number of times," Captain Amodh responded in a candid manner.

"Anyway, nothing to worry about now. We have already started her treatment. She will have to be here at least for next two days By the way, when are you going back to India?"

"Day after tomorrow night." It was a quick, short reply from Sushil.

"Well, I suggest you better postpone your return by minimum two to three days because even if discharged from here, she won't be able to take the long journey back home," the doctor opined.

"Okay, we will change our tickets accordingly. Can we see my wife now?" Captain Amodh inquired.

"Sorry. It's 8 pm already and visiting hours are over. You may come back at 11 am tomorrow. But only one person can see her at a time, remember that. Now, please excuse me. I have a lot of other jobs to do." The doctor left for his duty room without waiting for a reply.

The streets of the business districts of Bangkok boast of numerous Indian restaurants, that too with regional delicacy options. Punjabi dhabas, South Indian platter joints, specialised dosa corners, the works. While strolling back to their hotel, they picked out an upscale looking North Indian restaurant and walked inside for dinner. A pint of beer for Amodh, Mojitos for the three and plateful of tasty chicken tikkas helped all of them to come out of their gloominess. Leaving aside Manju's sickness, over sumptuous food they chatted generally and also discussed shopping in this beautiful city. They finally reached the hotel lobby around 11 pm. Just before heading for their rooms, Sushil gently nudged his father-in-law from behind. As Amodh turned, Sushil quickly whispered in his ears, "Papaji, please don't mind. Payal and I are going out now to see the night life here. And please don't worry; we will take care of ourselves. See you all tomorrow morning at the breakfast table. Good night."

Before Amodh could react or say something, the young couple had walked out of the hotel. They both boarded the Uber cab waiting by the roadside and sped off. "What happened Amodhji? Where are they going now, so late in the night?" Sujata looked genuinely concerned.

"Oh, don't bother. They have gone out to enjoy the evening." Amodh gave a short reply.

"Evening? It is past 11 now; you call that evening! Please don't try to cover up. I won't be able to get sleep the whole night. It's so scary!"

"Sujata ma'am, please don't take unnecessary tension. Let's do one thing. Let's just go to our rooms, freshen up and come back here to the lobby after fifteen minutes. There is a night bazaar nearby. Let's visit that and spend time shopping for our families. Then, we will go to a South Indian joint for a cup of good filter coffee. I know you love filter coffee a lot, isn't it?"

"So, you won't tell me where they have gone," Sujata sounded adamant.

"As I said, let's meet here after fifteen minutes," Amodh spoke in typical military officer's tone. That was enough to calm Sujata down, perhaps for the time being. She looked at him and started towards her room.

They met in the lobby, not after fifteen, but after twenty-five minutes. Sujata decided not to ask Amodh anything about her son and daughter-in-law, especially after his rather stern reply. But she did not like it at all. She had the right to know their whereabouts, especially in a foreign land, that too late at night. She followed him out of the hotel premises with a serious face.

Amodh, on the other hand, was also not feeling at ease with himself. He should not have spoken to her so harshly. But how could he tell her exactly where the young couple had gone! He finally decided to tell her the truth, but a little while later, and in his own typical manner.

They both walked to the night bazaar silently. The market was dazzling with bright LED lights of all shapes and sizes. Lavish display of colourful clothes and local decorative items made the market look very inviting. Customers, mainly foreigners, were busy bargaining and exchanging pleasantries. The place was brimming with life.

Women all over the world are supposed to be born shopaholics! But Sujata definitely was not in the correct frame of mind tonight.

Men are mostly terrible shoppers. Amodh was no exception. He always restricted his shopping to undergarments for himself. And especially today, with Manju languishing in the hospital and his darling daughter not around, he decided not to buy anything. Maybe he would revisit the place some other night.

After about half an hour of wasting time, they finally

left the market area for the hotel without buying anything for anyone. Just a little ahead but on the other side of the road, they came across a small South Indian restaurant. Crossing the road, especially for Sujata, proved a bit difficult as vehicular traffic was seemingly endless. After initial hesitation, when he found a relatively empty stretch, Amodh suddenly took her hand and just dashed towards the other side. It was done in a matter-of-fact manner, so Sujata didn't mind it. Instead, once seated inside the restaurant and after regaining her breath, she thanked him for the helping hand.

After ordering filter coffee and typical south Indian onion samosas, Amodh finally decided to break the hour-long silence. "Madam, I'm extremely sorry for speaking to you in a harsh tone. But believe me, I did so because I didn't know how to tell you where they have gone."

"Are you going to tell me now? Sujata enquired.

"Yes, of course. I'm fifty-seven years old now. I should not be asking your age but you are a married lady, a mom and a mother-in-law...."

"Don't feel shy to ask me that. I'm fifty-three now and I'm not embarrassed about it. At our present ages, we can discuss a lot of things which we otherwise could not have even imagined discussing as teenagers," Sujata interjected with a smile on her face.

"Yes, Sujata ji, very rightly said. At our age, we can

easily discuss problems encountered by ladies during menopause, breast cancer and issues related to men's bladder disorder etc. By the way, I am sure you know what Bangkok is famous for and why tourists from all over the world throng this place in herds!"

"Yeah, I know. Please go ahead," Sujata encouraged him.

"Well, to cut it short, it is famous for sex tourism. There are three main places in this city where such activities, I mean sex related shows go on—Patpong, Soi Cowboy and Nana-Plaza. Our children have gone to enjoy the show at one of these places. As we are staying in this Sukhumvit Road area, I guess they have gone to nearby Nana-Plaza. So, just don't worry, they will be back soon." Amodh heaved a sigh of relief after blurting out this information to the lady.

"Oh, I see! Amodhji, we are close relatives now; you could have told me this one hour back also. And to be honest, I have heard a lot about Bangkok's night life from my friends and colleagues back home. We are mature people so I can tell you this. I also wanted to go and see the show, but obviously along with my hubby. In fact, I had made some secret plans for both of us to sneak out from the hotel late in the night and head for one such show. I'm very inquisitive to see what actually happens there. I wish Sunil was here with all of us on this trip,"

Sujata confessed with a touch of sadness.

Momentarily, Amodh's cheeks became red with embarrassment. He never expected the otherwise very shy and reserved Sujata to suddenly express herself so boldly. Regaining his composure after a while, he commented, "Actually, I also wanted to see the show at least once in my lifetime. In fact, during my service in the Navy, I have visited Pattaya Port on a number of occasions. I believe a few such joints are there too. But being a senior officer on board the ship, I decided not to venture out to such places as I did not wish to be seen by my subordinate officers or sailors. And this time around also, unfortunately Manju's health has played spoilsport. Anyway, never mind, some other time, maybe!"

"Yes, I guess so!" Sujata's short comment brought the discussion on the sensuous topic to a close.

Having thoroughly enjoyed the unique taste of filter coffee and plateful of light snacks in the meanwhile, Amodh cleared the bill and was ready to go back to their hotel. But for that, they both had to cross the busy road once again. Unlike the last time, Amodh gripped Sujata's right hand firmly and approached the road. She did not object. He started looking towards the approaching vehicles. After a while, finding a reasonable gap between the speeding cars and buses, he sped across with Sujata in tow.

Screech... a superfast taxi appeared from nowhere and came to a sudden halt, probably just a few centimetres away from the duo. Both Amodh and Sujata had a miraculous escape; they found themselves suddenly stranded in front of the taxi, shell-shocked!

The driver put the blinking parking lights on and got down from the taxi. Instead of hurling abuses and screaming at them, the middle-aged Thai driver came and hugged both of them.

"Sorry! Very sorry, I not see you. Going where now? I drop you. Please allow." He honestly apologised to them in broken English.

"We are going back to our hotel close by. Thank you for the offer. But you drive so fast, you almost killed us!" Amodh replied in an agitated tone.

"I'm very sorry again! So now please allow me to serve you. You not going back to hotel. You now go for Patpong show. I take you there, wait and drop you back at hotel here. Taxi charges 1000 Baht. But I your friend now, I charge only 300 Baht. Very, very cheap. Patpong show very good! You, Indian family, no? So, please enjoy! Not waste time. Come, come! Quick." The driver opened the rear door and nearly pushed Amodh inside his cab. The gentlemanly Thai driver seemed to feel really very apologetic about the near crash. Otherwise he would have definitely charged a fortune for the same trip from others.

Amodh was still holding Sujata's hand. He quickly glanced at her. Her hand pushed his clasped hand towards the taxi. It was a silent and instant approval. It was a godsent opportunity for both of them. At least that's what they both thought!

Once seated inside the taxi, Sujata nudged him urging him to let go her hand. He released it immediately. Enough of hand holding! It was for a purpose; but so much had happened in the last few minutes that he had forgotten to release her hand. He felt sorry about it. He looked at her and gently smiled.

It was a quiet journey to Patpong district which lasted nearly half an hour. Well, not entirely quiet. Mr Throng, the driver, continued speaking with his rib-tickling English, explaining to them whatever possible about the tourist attractions in and around the city. He also took time out to enlighten them a bit about the shows they were going to see very shortly. Both passengers decided to keep absolutely quiet throughout Throng's monologue; but that did not deter him at all.

As per Mr Throng's directions, they paid for the entrance tickets and quickly entered the arena of the best show.

Though Captain Amodh Tiwari and Mrs Sujata Popli gained entry as a couple, they were still two different, independent individuals, married to two different persons. Sudden 'on-road' developments and their half-hearted willingness had brought them together. But standing together, what they started feeling was very baffling, mysterious, bewildering, strange, weird and inexplicable!

It was very embarrassing for both of them to watch the show together. Though both were standing next to each other, they chose not to have any eye contact. After about fifteen minutes into the strictly-for-adults show something terrible happened….

"Mummy! What are you doing here?"

"Papaji! You too? Both of you together, here?"

Suddenly hearing very loud, surprised, easily recognisable voices, both Sujata and Amodh turned around together.

Sushil and Payal were standing just in front of them! They had a terrible mix of expressions on their faces—of disbelief, shock and anger. Oh my God!

Sujata was dumbfounded! Her face suddenly became bright red with embarrassment! She started looking towards her own feet. Captain Amodh Kumar Tiwari, otherwise a tough-nut veteran officer of Indian Navy started trembling with guilt and shame!

"I'm asking you both once again! What are you people doing here together?" Sushil demanded to know, very agitated.

"What a shame Papa! *Chhee*!" Payal could not control her emotions too.

"Mota Bhai, please listen to me. Actually we both were crossing the ....."

"Enough of it, Papa. Please don't try to come up with some silly excuses. No need! You have already crossed the line, you know it well." Payal angrily interrupted her papa's meek explanation.

Amodh became speechless. Sujata was so shell-shocked that she just stood there and never tried to open her mouth!

"How can you both come to see such a show together? Your sacred relationship does not permit you that, does it, Papa? So how could you even think of doing such a thing? You were my ideal till this very moment but not anymore!" Payal's scolding hit her dear papa very hard, like a tight slap across his face. He stood motionless.

"We are a newly married couple, so came here to enjoy. But we're leaving this place right now! You both continue to enjoy. And you, my beloved mother! How disgusting!" Sushil took his wife's hand and left the viewing gallery in a huff.

Feeling stranded on a small island in the middle of an ocean, Amodh and Sujata looked at each other with dismay and quickly, quietly, left the show. What they had once considered as a godsent opportunity had turned out to be a total disaster, just an hour later!

It was not very difficult to find Throng at the taxi-stand. "Hello sir! Finished! So quick," Throng enquired while switching on the ignition, feeling genuinely surprised. But Amodh chose not to reply. "Hotel, please," is all he muttered.

Sushil and Payal asked us those pointed questions but what were they both doing there? Wasn't it shameful for both of them too! Amodh was asking himself, deliberately trying to clear his clouded mind. Of course not! They are a young, married couple now. They can always go for such things. But not us, me and Sujataji! Definitely not. Oh God! How on earth could we both commit such a blunder? What a disgraceful act on my part, first time ever! God please forgive me.

In the rear seat near the other window Sujata sat absolutely motionless, her mind totally blank! She had stopped thinking! Tears were rolling down her cheeks.

The next morning in a genuine effort to clear things Amodh wrote a longish WhatsApp message explaining the circumstances which had landed him and Sujata in Patpong area. He sent the message to both Payal and Sushil. But he never received any reply from either of them! Both the children had become painfully silent!

Manju recovered fully and came out of the hospital three days later. Amodh went to the hospital every morning to see her. And Sujata went to see her during the evening visiting hours. For the complimentary buffet breakfast, they sat at different tables and had other meals in their own rooms. They both avoided coming face to face with each other. Probably it had dawned on them what a terrible social crime they had committed, albeit in the heat of the moment, without any ulterior motive and without realising the consequences!

The families came back to India four days later than the original schedule. Sushil and Payal nearly stopped speaking with Sujata and Amodh. However, in front of others, not to raise any suspicion, they tried to behave somewhat normally.

In order to speak at length and sort out the misunderstanding, Amodh invited the young couple to the club a number of times but Sushil always gave some lame excuses to call off the meeting. Payal generally avoided speaking with her dear papa. She always felt that her dad had committed a heinous crime in Bangkok. Probably he had some other sinister plans for her mother-in-law that night! He was all alone in the hotel room, after all! She could never imagine that her beloved, respected dad could ever do such a terrible thing, that too with her mother-in-law! Payal could never forgive him.

In the other household, forget about speaking, Sushil almost stopped looking at his own mother. He also could never think that his loving, docile mom could ever commit such a shameful act.

Four odd months later, one fine day, without giving prior warning to their parents, Sushil and Payal left for New Zealand, for good! Soon after coming back from that fateful Thailand trip, they had quietly applied to New Zealand High Commission for immigration.

Mr Sunil Popli and Mrs Manju Tiwari felt terribly heartbroken with their son and daughter's sudden, unannounced departure. They failed to understand the actual reason behind such a drastic decision taken by their children. Sushil was such a caring son! How could he suddenly decide to leave his parents and move to a faraway land, that too for good? On the other hand, Payal, a typical Fauji's daughter, loved her motherland a lot, probably more than anybody else. How come she too decided to desert her beloved country?

Unknown to Sunil and Manju, Amodh and Sujata guessed the actual reason behind such a bold and drastic decision taken by the young couple. They have been repenting their adventurous move that fateful night ever since. They could never ever make proper eye contact with each other!

The Bangkok fiasco had taken its toll!

Love You / Love You Not

"Hello Vijay uncle! I'm Rehan speaking."

"Good morning Rehan. It's 4 o'clock in the morning, beta. Why are you calling me up at this hour? Hope everything is alright at home!" Vijay had sat up on his bed startled.

"No uncle, Papa has just expired. Oh Papa...!" Rehan could not control himself and he broke down on the phone.

"Oh my God! What are you saying? I spoke to him just two days back; he was sounding hale and hearty. What happened?" Vijay was shocked.

"Uncle, it was a sudden heart attack. Please come soon," a completely shattered Rehan hung up on him.

Vijay Mote and Rushad Dinshaw were childhood friends. They lived in the same Lokhandwala complex in Andheri West area of Mumbai, had gone to the same government school for studies in the mornings and to the same playground for playing cricket in the afternoons. They played together, loafed around together, fought with other boys together and studied together before the exams. So much so that after attaining adolescence they chased the same girl together! After graduating from the same college, Vijay got employed in a private company in nearby Borivali area. So he, along with his parents, continued staying in the same Lokhandwala complex. After a year or so, his dear friend Rushad got married to a very rich girl and shifted to Colaba in South Mumbai. This happened almost two decades ago.

His wife Neeta and their only daughter Vinita were out of town. Vijay got ready in fifteen minutes and started his car for the southernmost tip of this great city Mumbai, the city of opportunities. The traffic should be very thin at this time of the day and he expected to reach Rushad's home in an hour's time. While negotiating the turns and curves, vehicles and criss-crossing pedestrians efficiently, Vijay got lost in his own thoughts. Sheela, Rushad's wife for last twenty-odd years, must be in a terrible state of mind now. He distinctly remembered the day he and Rushad met her in college for the very first time....

...It was the college day festival, their very first one. A whole lot of students of all seniority and streams were dancing in pairs, the famous Gujarati Garba dance. LGBT were uncommon and not publicly accepted in those days. But still there were happy, laughing female pairs and very unhappy with themselves (unsuccessful lechers!) male pairs dancing in the melee too! Most of them were in no way connected to future LGBT movement! Vijay and Rushad belonged to that disgusted second category! With very loud background music, the dancing partners could not hear each other. So, they were just smiling and following one another's dance moves. All of them were moving in a big circle and also revolving around themselves once in a while. During one such rotational movement, suddenly there was a power cut, which is very rare in Mumbai. And before anybody could scream in despair *'Oh! Teri Ma ki!'*, Vijay received a solid blow on his nose. In the pitch darkness, he held his bleeding nose and screamed, "Oh sister-f……" Moments later, the electricity supply was automatically restored. Lo and Behold! There was an astonished, pretty girl standing in front of him, casually holding a Garba stick very close to his already broken nose! The culprit was instantly identified and caught almost red-handed!

"Oh! I'm extremely sorry. The lights went off the moment I whirled inward so I couldn't see you at all. It's all my fault. Please forgive me," the girl pleaded guilty and also for instant pardon.

If the defaulter had been a boy, Vijay and Rushad would have beaten him up black and blue. And probably as a parting return gift, they would have broken his nose too! But here they both probably sensed an opportunity, a romantic one at that. So, they just smiled at her—that cute, 'It's okay, it's all my fault' type innocent smile.

"Hi! I'm Sheela, Sheela Soda Bottle Opener Wala. You're bleeding profusely. Maybe the nose is fractured! I've a car. Let's go to the hospital quickly. Please don't refuse."

Vijay somehow managed to hold back his laugh. What a funny surname! Wow! But being a Parsi, Rushad was not feeling amused. "Never mind. There is a medical tent with a doctor inside the college ground itself; I'll take him there. By the way, I'm Rushad Dinshaw and he is my childhood friend Vijay Mote," he immediately replied.

Sheela shook hands and accompanied both of them to the doctor's tent. Luckily, though he was in pain his nose was not fractured!

There is a proverb—no pain, no gain. Vijay's pain gained the instant affection of Sheela for him. Vijay belonged to a typical lower middle-class family. On the other hand, Sheela belonged to an affluent Parsi family living in a posh house in upscale Colaba. She always moved around in a chauffeur driven Merc. But otherwise, she was a fairly mature, practical girl for her age. She befriended both the boys and secretly observed their personal traits over the next few months. Finally, she fell for Vijay, probably because of his simplicity and IQ. Men always fall for external beauty of women, whereas women look for inner beauty in men!

It's not that Sheela didn't find any good qualities in Rushad. She was quite friendly with him as well, but preferred to spend more time with Vijay alone. Both friends fought with each other over her a few times. Rushad felt heartbroken and jealous for losing a beautiful girl from his own community to his dearest friend. But after some time, he accepted his defeat and became Sheela's 'other best friend'. So Rushad and Vijay continued to remain good friends.

During the next year's college fest, Rushad suffered from pneumonia and had to stay back at home. By then Sheela had fallen deeply in love with Vijay. Maybe she wanted to make up for last year's mishap of nearly breaking his nose so, during the fest, she took him to her home one day. Her parents had gone to Gujarat for a few days so no one was at home except the security guard outside. There Sheela and Vijay secretly made love with each other. It was the first time and the only time for both of them!

After graduating from the college a year later, Vijay, being from a needy family, decided to give up further studies and look for a job instead. And after getting employment, he, very sheepishly but at the same time very expectantly proposed to Sheela. She was more than willing but her parents played spoilsports! Unlike those third-rate Hindi film stories, it was not because of a rich-poor gap. Sheela's parents wanted their only daughter to get married to someone from their extremely close-knit community only. Sheela tried her best to convince them but failed. Finally, she decided to marry Rushad, her other good friend in the college. Rushad belonged to a lower middle class family too, but he was from Sheela's community. So her parents had no valid reasons to reject him! And Rushad was so thrilled with the unexpected, terrific, life-changing proposal that he chose to completely overlook and ignore Vijay's closeness with Sheela. Well, he didn't know anything about their secret close physical encounter! No one knew!

However, after the marriage, the geographical distance between two childhood friends increased considerably as Rushad moved to his in-law's palatial house in South Mumbai. Vijay, quite a mature man, maintained very cordial friendship with both. In these twenty long years, they did get occasional opportunities to come very close to each other. But both Sheela and Vijay maintained the sanctity of their triangular friendship and never ever crossed the limit.

The road to Colaba really had very thin traffic. Vijay reached his late friend's house in forty-five minutes. The mortal remains of his dear friend were kept in the spacious drawing room. Sheela, wearing a pure white cotton salwar suit was sitting next to her husband's head. She sat there absolutely motionless and speechless, simply continuing to stare at her dear husband's expressionless face!

Vijay tiptoed across the room and sat next to her. Seeing him, she instantly hugged him and broke down on his broad shoulder. He decided not to ask her any questions and silently comforted her. 'How' and 'When' didn't really matter now. His childhood buddy Rushad had already left this world! Left for good!

Rushad's body was taken to the Tower of Silence that afternoon for a typical Parsi burial. Not allowed to enter, Vijay patiently waited outside for the ritual to get over. He then accompanied Sheela and Rehan back to Colaba, had tea before setting course for Lokhandwala. He reached back home by late evening. While having tea, not Sheela but her son Rehan had narrated what had actually happened.

Though a casual beer drinker otherwise, Rushad had developed a penchant for expensive liquor after his marriage and moving into Sheela's rich household. Smoking was his favourite pastime since teenage days. Over a period of time, Rushad had become a heavy drinker and a chain smoker. For the last two days, he had been feeling uneasiness and mild chest pain. But both Rushad and Sheela ignored it thinking it was acidity, from which, of late, he had been suffering very frequently. Last night, Rushad woke up around 4 am, went to the toilet and came back soon after. Nearing the bed, he suddenly collapsed and fell flat on the floor. A sudden, massive heart attack had done him in! There was no chance of any revival. He had fallen on the soft and thick bedside rug, so did not get injured physically. External injuries, minor or major, do not matter for a dead man anyway!

About two weeks later, Sheela called up Vijay and requested him to come over for some consultation. That was the first time she actually and directly spoke to him after Rushad's untimely death. By then, both Neeta and Vinita were back in Mumbai. So, to keep up the social etiquette, Vijay decided to take them along. He considered it proper for his entire family to visit the bereaved family to pay their heartfelt condolences formally.

Vijay since his marriage had been providing all possible comforts to Neeta but could never fall in love with her. On her part, Neeta was extremely short-tempered and always suspected Vijay of having an extramarital affair with someone, somewhere. Neeta also disliked Sheela, the extrovert, filthy rich and extremely beautiful woman who always appeared to be unnecessarily extra-friendly with her husband. At the same time, she envied her too! And maybe merely for vengeance, Neeta chose to become a close friend of Rushad! Obviously, that was not appreciated by Sheela either. With such varied feelings, relations between the families were not that good especially between these two women. But there was a silver lining in the black clouds. Seventeen-year old Vinita and 19-year-old Rehan, like their respective fathers, had also become close childhood friends! And that's why, after coming back from a short holiday with her mom in Delhi, Vinita insisted on meeting Rehan.

The visiting family was ushered into the drawing room. After a while, both Sheela and Rehan appeared from their bedrooms to meet up with the guests.

"Hello Sheela! I'm so very sorry and upset to know about Rushad's untimely death! He was so full of life, so energetic, so very friendly! I'm at a loss for words!" Neeta confessed, holding Sheela's hands.

Sheela momentarily forgot all animosity and embraced Neeta tightly. They sobbed in each other's arms for a while. Rehan and Vinita too hugged each other and cried.

After having tea and snacks Sheela cleared her throat and started the main topic of their informally arranged meeting. "Vijay, you know that after my dad's death, Rushad was managing our generations-old bakery business quite nicely. But now, with him gone forever, there is no one to look after that."

"Yes, of course I know that. So what are your plans?" Vijay asked.

"Well, ideally speaking, Rehan should take over the business immediately. But he is only nineteen now and yet to complete graduation. Moreover, he is not at all business minded we all know. Also, after graduation he wants to do MBA, maybe from USA. That means someone else will have to look after it for the next five odd years at least," Sheela spoke thoughtfully.

"Then how are you going to manage it?"

"I really don't know. That's why I requested you to come here," Sheela admitted.

"Thanks for reposing faith in me but you must have planned something."

"Honestly, no plans. But as there is no trustworthy person around, I'm left with no choice but to jump into it all by myself. And I don't even have my dear mom alive to give me some moral support! I can't manage it alone," Sheela stated simply.

"You can always keep a manager, a good one," Neeta interjected.

"Neeta, it's a question of trust and faith. I was thinking of asking your husband to be a part of this business."

Everyone suddenly fell silent in the room. Vijay felt flabbergasted. He was trying to think quickly but before he could decide on what to speak, Neeta pulled at his shirt. He got the hint. It was actually a stern warning, 'Be careful!' He nodded and spoke up slowly, "I don't know what exactly you are offering me. A manager's post or partnership in your business."

Sheela smiled after a long time. "I know you've a well-paying job. So why should I offer you another job? That too a low-paying one!"

"Then what Sheela?" Vijay sounded eager to know.

"Vijay, I have already confessed I don't really have any proposal for you. That's why we all need to sit and discuss as to how you can be part of your late friend's business. Can you think of something?" She urged.

Neeta pulled at his shirt once again. This time it was more forceful. It simply meant 'stop it'.

"Oh Sheela, it is a total surprise for me. I need some time to think it over. Can we talk about this after a few days? Maybe by then you will also think of and finalise some deal for me, so to say," Vijay wanted to cut short the discussion. He didn't wish to pick up an unnecessary fight with Neeta, in Sheela's house itself.

"Yeah, sure. Take your time. So, how was your Delhi trip Vinita? Met all your friends? Enjoyed or not?" Sheela changed the topic instantly.

After small talk on other unrelated subjects, Vijay and his small family left Colaba an hour later.

Neeta had no intention of allowing Vijay to get actively involved in Rushad's business. She presumed that would progressively make him extremely close to fiery, feisty Sheela. Neeta was actually scared of losing him permanently to her. So, while going back, she tried her level best to reason with him. "Vijay, I'm sorry to have signalled you to stop the discussion. But don't you think that leaving your present job suddenly is not a good idea at all. You are earning pretty well, isn't it?"

"That's right. But even if she offers me just ten to twelve per cent of the profit, that will be more than twice my salary."

"I know they have an old, well-established and flourishing business but there are so many uncertainties in business. Anything can happen anytime," Neeta argued angrily.

"Oh really! You think so! All established business houses always follow ethical practices. So if things are run honestly and in proper way, no business will ever collapse, take that from me."

"Okay, leave that aside. What about the distance? Can you drive for two hours one way to reach Colaba in the morning and two more hours in the evening to come back home?" She was not giving up.

"Why take so much pain? We can always shift to some area nearby; Kamathipura or Worli will be fine. What do you say?" Vijay appeared all set to join Sheela as a business partner, at least his arguments indicated that way.

"But what about Maaji and Babuji, I mean your old parents? How about our flat! Do we sell it off? And what about Vinita's education? You know how difficult it is for a child to get admission in a college here. It is like getting into IAS!" Neeta sounded terribly agitated and desperate.

"Neeta, in today's world, people change jobs like they change clothes, that too for a pittance of a raise. If Sheela gives me a reasonably lucrative offer, then why not shift our household and start a new life! I'm already a manager in my company. There is no further growth. They will not offer me any post in the Board of Directors any time, no way! So, I'll retire from the company after another ten-twelve years, in the present post only. On the other hand, if the offer from Sheela is really good then we can even think of putting Vinita in that expensive college of Rehan. Don't you wish to become rich some day?"

All this while Vinita had been listening to her parents' discussions very intently. She now suddenly became an active participant. "Oh Papa, that's a fantastic college to be in! And my dear Mom, please get rid of all your negativity and think positive, at least once in your life!" Vinita was very fond of Rehan, probably loved him. She didn't wish to lose this golden opportunity of going to the same college as him.

Vijay burst out laughing. He was genuinely amused. On her part, Neeta made a grumpy face and stared outside. She had lost the battle! She was fuming inside.

Vijay suddenly felt very sad and missed his old friend Rushad quite a lot. They had grown up together! But the prospect of winning back Sheela, his 'lost love' grossly overshadowed all sorrows of life! He was thus quite keen to join her business ASAP. But at the same time, he wanted to bargain and secure a good financial package for himself. Mumbai is the most expensive city of India, after all!

He had a fair idea about the total annual earnings of Sheela's family business. Marked skyward changes in Rushad's post-marriage lifestyle had said it all. He knew that anything higher than 15 per cent of the net profit was a welcome deal. As a good marketing strategist, he patiently waited for the offer to come from Sheela first. She finally called up after two days on a Sunday afternoon! Vijay had been waiting very patiently and it paid off.

"Hi Vijay! How are you? Have you given it a thought? Time is running out for me, in fact for all of us!"

"Hi Sheela, nice to hear your melodious voice. Yes, I've thought about the whole thing. Let me clarify a few things about joining you, I mean your business. Firstly, in order to get actively involved in it on a regular basis, I will have to sell off our present flat in Lokhandwala and move permanently to a place much closer to you. This is going to be tedious job and will involve a lot of money. Then Vinita's college has to be changed, though only for a year. And finally, I'm a bit apprehensive about leaving a secure job and jumping into a totally new thing, that too at such a late stage! The very survival of my entire family including my old parents is at stake. I'm really very scared Sheela!"

"Vijay; we are best friends, isn't it? I know that once involved, you will give more than 100 per cent to the business. And, unlike Rushad, you are not into heavy drinking. So, just trust me, things will become alright. Now tell me have you thought about the financial part?"

"No, not really. You know my present financial state and the stakes. So, let's be very open and frank about it. Tell me first, what's in your mind!"

"Vijay, I know that you don't have money to invest. But honestly, with almighty God's blessings, I don't require any financial assistance to run the business now. If you run the business as per my directions, I mean just peripheral advice from time to time; I think I can give you one-fifth of the net profit. So basically you will not be the business partner, but the CEO with twenty per cent profit of the company as your salary, sorry, the annual package. And with time and your hard work, as the company profit soars, so will be your package. So friend, what do you say about it?"

"Oh, I'm impressed with your business acumen! I'm not a partner because I don't have capital to invest; and I'm not a salaried manager either. But I'm the manager who finally takes home a part of the profit. But how will that be because I have no idea!" Vijay feigned complete ignorance.

"Come on Vijay have faith in me. I know how much you get these days, Rushad had told me once. In today's scenario, the offer I've made will definitely give you minimum double of that amount. So chill."

"Sheela, can I say something now?"

"Yes, of course! Let's both of us be very straightforward about it. Please go ahead," she replied.

"Well, in that case, I'll request you to please make it one-fourth in place of one-fifth. That will be just five per cent increase in the package for me, which is obviously peanuts for you! And secondly, may I ask you to sanction a long-term official advance; I mean a loan of about 25 lac rupees immediately. This will ensure a quick and smooth relocation for my family. We all know how expensive things are in Mumbai. You may deduct one lac rupees per month from my salary towards interest free payback. If you kindly agree to these two proposals, then I'm all yours!" Vijay deliberately made a suggestive comment.

Sheela thought for a while, ignored his hint and gave a business like reply. "Okay Vijay! Let's make it 23 per cent, full and final. Also, I'll give you Rs 25 lacs upfront loan straightaway. This amount can be repaid by you per month without any interest. I'm sure that will bring a smile to your grumpy face. Now please tell me when can you join, how soon? I'm in a hurry because right now no one is monitoring the business!"

"Thank you, Madam! I'll be delighted to work with you. And let me just clarify that we are not on a video call so you can't see my facial expressions! Now, I'll give one week's notice to my present boss, hope he agrees. And then I can join you the very next day. But in case he wants me to give minimum one month's notice, then I'll be stuck very badly! Everything will get delayed thereafter."

"I know the corporate game very well here. If not more, they will obviously ask you to give clear one month's notice, failing which they will deduct that month's salary. What I suggest is that you resign tomorrow itself without giving any advance notice. And on your behalf, our company will compensate them financially. You join our company the very next day, that's from Tuesday. Till you finalise and buy a flat nearby to shift in, you must come to office daily travelling the long distance smilingly, whether you like it or not. And Vijay, let me make one thing very clear right in the beginning—we are going to have a strictly business relationship with each other, and nothing more. So let's forget about our past relations please, I beg of you!"

Vijay felt a little hurt hearing her stern admonition and the subsequent pleading. Why is Sheela behaving like this? She is a free bird now. But he loved her very deeply, and come what may, he would continue to love her. So, he chose to ignore it. She will definitely come around one day. So, let me be just slow and steady for now, he thought.

The management was very upset and angry with Vijay for his sudden decision to quit the company, that too without giving any proper notice. After all, it is a lengthy and tedious process to search for and recruit an efficient and honest employee, that too a manager. However, the blank cheque sent by Sheela through a supervisor somewhat took care of their anger and ensured an easy exit for Vijay.

Within the ensuing two months, Vijay and his family, including his parents, sold off their old flat in Lokhandwala and shifted to a small flat in Worli. And he got well settled in his new job too. Under his expert control and monitoring, Sheela's bakery business witnessed a quick turnaround. Sheela was extremely happy with his performance as a sincere, good manager. It is high time I start pleasing my boss, Vijay thought and got into the act of wooing Sheela very seriously. He was a romantic but not a poetic person. He knew that Sheela loved and appreciated artistic creativity, especially romantic poems. So, WhatsApp came to his rescue. Bishu Varghese, an old friend, regularly wrote and posted *shayaris* (poetry) in their 'Lokhandi Boyz' group. Vijay started to religiously copy Bishu's shayari every day and sent it to Sheela. When it landed on Sheela's mobile, instead of 'Forwarded', it actually appeared as an original poem written by Vijay. Initially, she just read the shayari, smiled and ignored it. Bishu mainly wrote romantic couplets, and though a Malayali Christian by birth, he wrote rather well. Sheela appreciated Vijay's sincere efforts to write such poems exclusively for her. However, she neither acknowledged nor replied back with any remarks, not even with a simple 'Good morning' message. Unfazed, Vijay continued to post a 'Good morning Sheela' message to her almost immediately followed by shayari by about nine o'clock every morning, without fail. As expected and anticipated by him, after a while it became a habit for Sheela. She actually started looking out for his good morning messages and his original shayari! Creating artificial demand is a great marketing strategy!

After forty days, Vijay took a calculated risk and stopped sending any message to her. Sheela was a little surprised. Maybe he is busy today or just forgot about it, she thought and decided to ignore. But when no messages came from Vijay the next day also, she got worried. Though she had imposed strict self-control upon herself and steadfastly ignored all advances from Vijay for all these days, she did like his romantic poems and his devotion towards her. She just did not wish to lose him!

'Good morning. No poems today!' She couldn't control herself anymore and messaged him.

Vijay's patience had finally paid off. He had been eagerly waiting for this since the previous day. He immediately messaged back, 'Good morning Sheela. I thought you did not like my poems because you never responded.'

'No, the poems are really nice. You actually wrote these yourself! Seriously?'

'So you like my poems but not me! That's very unfair!' Vijay replied, skilfully skirting her question.

'Hey! Please don't start off again. We had an understanding, isn't it?'

'What understanding Sheela? It was just a one-sided dictat from you, and I don't know why.'

'Please send the poem as and when you write next, if you so desire. Thanks. Bye.'

Vijay realised their chat was heading for a dead-end. So he quickly texted, 'Sure. But can we meet sometime, somewhere? Just the two of us. Please….'

'Hmm…why not? We are college time friends. You can always come home to meet me. Come tomorrow, maybe after lunch,' Sheela replied after making Vijay wait for half an hour.

'Ok, thanks a lot Boss. See you tomorrow.' He exited the chat and entered the manager's cabin. Like many other educated, well-placed people, he too had been texting while driving from home to his office! We, the incorrigible Indians!

Vijay finished his lunch a little early the next day, briefed his supervisor thoroughly and left for Sheela's house. She was sitting in her spacious drawing room, probably waiting for him. But she was not alone. Bruno was sitting next to her looking towards the entrance door, saliva drooling from his long, loosely hanging tongue. Bruno was Sheela's 12-year-old pet dog.

This was his first visit to her house in two months. He badly wanted to win her back.

"Sheela, sorry, last time we couldn't speak with each other freely as Neeta was around. It's really very nice to see that you're looking quite bright and fresh today. Dear friend Rushad's untimely death was tragic! Good to see that you are coming out of it slowly."

"You know Vijay, I was very much aware that he was heading for it. So much of drinking and smoking cannot take you anywhere else, you see! Nobody can ever help a person who does not wish to help himself. I have failed to understand what his compulsions were! Wasn't he happy with me?"

"Sorry to say this about my good old friend, that too who is no longer alive, but maybe he couldn't handle it the right way; I mean all of a sudden becoming so wealthy, so powerful as the boss of the company, just after marrying you. Everyone can't handle instant name and famc, you see! There are examples galore, especially in the film industry."

"Oh! I never considered that factor. You're probably right, Vijay. I used to think that he was unable to forget his ex-flame or something. Many times I did think of asking you but never did so. Was he seeing someone before our marriage?"

"No, he never had any girlfriend, I swear! And I don't really know much about any casual sex he may have had with someone earlier. But after the marriage, you were the only woman in his life, that's for sure. Trust me!"

"Thanks for that info, for clearing my doubts. Now tell me, what exactly brings you here? Any official matter?"

"Of course not! All those are sorted out telephonically, I mean by talking to you on the mobile. Hey! I think it is high time we coined a new word for it, 'Mobilly'! Talking on telephones–Telephonically; talking on mobiles–Mobilly! Well, how is it?"

"Terrible! One of your poorest jokes. A stinking one!" Sheela laughed while giving her honest verdict.

"I was dying to hear you laugh Sheela! I've been interacting with you very frequently for the last few months, especially after joining your business. Why have you stopped living, dear?" He stared straight into her big, black eyes, looking for an honest answer.

Sheela looked pained. She slowly shifted her gaze towards Bruno and then upwards towards the roof. Vijay followed her eyes and realised there were CCTV cameras fitted in each corner of the room.

"When did you install these cameras? And why? These were not there when we visited you last time," a surprised Vijay asked.

"Yes, you are right. These cameras were not fitted that time. Actually, the Vet has very recently detected a large tumour in Bruno's stomach. Due to unbearable pain, at times he coils up in any corner of the house and collapses. If you don't find him immediately and inject a pain-killer, he will die. That's why after consulting the Vet, we've installed this CCTV system all over the house, except inside the bedrooms of course, just to locate him. Rehan generally keeps monitoring the system all the while."

"Oh, I see! What about the garden?" Vijay inquired.

"No, because we don't let Bruno venture out there alone. Our maid takes him there in the evenings for some light exercises. It's not very hot today, so let's go to the garden and sit under the mango tree. What do you say?"

"Yes, of course! I was about to suggest the same. Let's rise and shine." Vijay took her hint and quickly got up.

After they both got settled in the garden, Vijay decided to bring back the topic. "So, my dear Sheela, please give me some reply! Why have you stopped living? You were so full of fun and life till a few months back. What has happened to you now? You have become so mechanical, so stiff these days!"

"Vijay, there are phases in everyone's life. I think the happy phase of my life is over now. Maybe God has punished me, made me a widow so early for the sin committed during our college days, between two of us." Sheela sounded quite sad, unhappy with herself.

"Hey, come on Sheela! We made love only once because we both were madly in love with each other! I don't know about your feelings but I still love you, and only you! They say first love can never be forgotten; I know how true that saying is!" Vijay paused for a few seconds and continued, "And for heaven sake, please stop blaming yourself for Rushad's untimely, unfortunate death. A few minutes back you only said that 'you knew it was coming'! And Sheela, you were born and brought up in a wealthy, progressive family in Mumbai, the most modern, liberal city of this country! And you have such an orthodox, should I say backward mindset? Feeling guilty for someone's natural death? Hey! Give me a break, please!"

"Vijay, wealth and surroundings can influence one's behaviour pattern, not the inner self. I think it was my sacred duty to inform my husband about our secret encounter before the wedding but I failed! As I sit alone at home most part of the day and the entire night, I just repent my actions because now, that is the only thing left for me to do!" She started sobbing softly.

Vijay got up from his chair and held her face with both hands. Making her look into his eyes, he pleaded, "Sheela, please stop blaming yourself unnecessarily. I'm not sure if God is actually there or not but believe me, even if God exists, He just does not have time to dictate individual lives of the entire human race! So, please try and come out of this self-created cocoon! You are still very young; so stop repenting and start living once again, I sincerely beg of you!"

Before Sheela could reply, Bruno's distinct growl forced Vijay to quickly reoccupy his chair. Dogs are quite possessive of their masters and physical closeness with any outsider makes them feel very insecure. Had he not retracted in time, Vijay would have got attacked by ailing Bruno. He did not wish to go back home with a torn black trouser and prominent dog bite marks on his bums!

"Bruno, take it easy. He is a friend!" Sheela pacified

Bruno and smiled at Vijay.

"Maybe you are right, Vijay. But somehow, I'm not able to forget things and forgive myself," she candidly admitted.

"Do you still love me Sheela?" Vijay took her right hand and suddenly asked.

Sheela appeared puzzled. She looked the other way and softly answered, "Vijay, please! Don't embarrass me with such questions."

"I think I've got your answer. You still love me; in fact, you never stopped loving me."

"No comments whatsoever!"

"And you also know very well that I never stopped loving you. I got married because of unbearable family pressure. And that ruined my entire life! Neeta is so damn suspicious of each and every move of mine! Right from our honeymoon, I don't think we have ever spent a single day without fighting! I'm so unhappily married!" It was Vijay's turn to weep.

In reply, neither did Sheela hold his chin up, nor did she wipe his tears. She just kept staring at him, waiting for him to calm down.

"I can sense almost everything about your family life, Vijay. I know she is an odd woman. But now you have no other choice but to live with her."

"No, Sheela, I don't wish to waste my life like this.

God has given us this opportunity to come close to each other once again so let's make a new life out of this! Let's reunite, please." Vijay literally begged her.

"Come on, don't be stupid and don't try to complicate your life! You have old parents and a teenage daughter living with you. And lastly, I'm not that same old Sheela anymore! My life has changed, changed for good. I'll continue to live a simple, detached, lonely life, with only one expectation—I want to see my loving son Rehan become a very successful entrepreneur, a big man. So, please don't try your old stunts with me!"

"Sheela, please don't insult my undying love for you by calling it a stunt; you hurt me!"

"Sorry! But please leave me alone."

"Yaar, all of us have got just one life to live! As the famous saying goes, 'Don't add days to your life, instead, add life to your days'. Please live your life, Sheela! Give life another chance!"

"I'm sorry Vijay, but since the time Rushad died, I've been remembering all the fights we used to have regularly over such trivial issues. And I feel guilty on all counts. I keep thinking about how, if I actually wished, we could have avoided such unpleasant happenings. Maybe I could have been more forceful in compelling him to leave drinking and smoking. But after a while I just gave up! Maybe he would have been still alive! All those things haunt me now!"

"Sheela, I'm requesting you once again, this time with folded hands, please get rid of such terrible thoughts! And please allow me to make you fall in love with me, all over again!"

"Get lost!" Sheela dismissed him summarily with a broad smile on her face.

"Okay, I'm leaving now. But I'll keep sending you the shayaris till you ask me to stop. Thanks for the coffee. Bye!" Vijay left leisurely, grinning.

'Good morning Sheela!' Vijay messaged her the next morning. There was no reply. So, half an hour later, his, sorry, Bishu Varghese's latest, fresh shayari duly followed:

'Nafraton ke bazaar mein
meri ek rehri hai mohabbat ki
Tum kuchh kharido ya nahin
mol bhao karne to aajao!'

(In this market of hatred… I've a cart of love
Whether you buy anything or not… at least come over to bargain!)

The return message finally came after five minutes in the form of a cute smiley. Vijay was thrilled with life; his day was made! Encouraged, he took the liberty to send her a romantic 'Good night' message just before hitting the bed that night. Sheela sent him back a simple 'Gud night' message.

The messaging saga continued between the two ex-lovers for many months. Bruno died sometime in between. Though Vijay started sending some sexy messages and soft proposals in between, Sheela stuck to just a smiley and a 'Gud Night'.

Neeta, on her part, was extremely unhappy with Vijay's decision to join Sheela's business. She was sure that they were having an affair. After trying very hard for a long time, one fateful night once Vijay started snoring under the influence of alcohol, she managed to unlock his mobile by using his finger. She was shocked to see her husband's numerous messages, shayaris and Sheela's short and sweet replies. Next morning the couple had a terrible fight, with Vijay vehemently refusing to accept any romantic involvement with Sheela. Neeta's suspicion was however, very strong. Feeling helpless, she slowly went into some kind of depression. Their quarrelling also continued unabated.

It was Navratri time. Visibly fed up with no further progress beyond messaging on the love front, Vijay finally decided to drive down to Colaba to meet Sheela, to wish her and also to propose to her, if possible. He wanted to divorce Neeta and start a new life with Sheela!

"Hello, my beautiful Boss! How's life?" he enquired after entering the house.

"Hi! I'm good. And what exactly brings you here? It's

not office work, I'm damn sure," she smilingly replied.

"Hey, Bruno is no longer alive but your CCTV system is still on monitoring each and every move of ours! Can we go to your bedroom to talk to each other a little freely?" Vijay was desperate.

"Yeah, we lost Bruno, so now the CCTV cameras are generally used to keep a check on the maids. By the way, right now I'm all alone in the house, all maids have gone. Can I really trust you?" Sheela mockingly asked.

"I really don't know. Please ask yourself!" Vijay replied in a sarcastic manner.

"Okay smarty! My bedroom toilet has another door opening into the dining area as well. You enter it through that door and I'll go to the bedroom a little later and open the other door to let you inside. It won't look proper on the CCTV system if we both walk into my bedroom together," Sheela whispered.

Vijay felt very excited. *My dream of our physical reunion is finally coming true*, he thought and gave enthusiastic thumbs up to her.

Once inside, Vijay almost lunged forward to embrace Sheela. She quickly stepped back and gave him a dirty look. Her cold stare disarmed him completely. He quietly occupied the chair kept in front of her dressing table.

"Vijay, I never expected this from you. I trusted you and genuinely thought you wanted to have a one-on-one chat with me, not monitored by the cameras. But this? Just not done!"

"I'm terribly sorry, but Sheela our relationship has become so stagnant! There is no progress at all!"

"I'm sure I clarified my stand almost a year ago. Please have no expectations from me. I like your shayaris and at the same time admire you as a nice person, that's all."

"Sheela, please don't cheat yourself! You're forty-three now and I'm sure you desperately need a man in your life! Give yourself another chance, Sheela!"

"Please let me live my life the way I want Vijay!"

"I'm having a terrible time at home. Not a single day passes without a fight! I'm fed up with life. I've decided to give Neeta a divorce as soon as possible. So, please accept me in your life, I beg of you my love!"

"Vijay, please calm down! I told you this one year back, and am once again telling you now, don't complicate so many lives. Time is the biggest healer. So, take things easy. Neeta will come around one day."

Vijay was proved wrong once again! Sheela indeed was not interested in him any longer! He was hurt but didn't wish to give up. So, he came close to her and whispered, "Do you still remember that afternoon during Navratri, twenty-two long years back, when we both became one, for the very first time? I can never forget that wonderful experience! Sheela, can we make love once again, today?

For heaven sake, don't say 'No'!"

"A big No to that! I think our conversation is not going in the right direction. So, before you lose your self-control and jump over me once again, let's call it a day and go outside. I can't take any more chances with you!" Sheela was very stern in her reply.

"Yaar, I've already apologised to you. I'm not going to do anything stupid now! But before going back to my horrible wife to face her terrible temper, can I request you for a hug at least? A friendly hug!"

Sheela didn't mind that. So, they got up and embraced each other. Vijay held her tightly and planted a few kisses on her forehead, eyes, cheeks in quick successions and approached her lips. Sheela was expecting this, so she immediately turned her face away. "That's enough for next one year! Now go home and celebrate Navratri," she smilingly pushed him away.

"Madam, you've been rejecting my love, time and again! Never mind, one day you will say 'Yes' and come back to me, I swear!" Vijay made a famous Shahrukh Khan pose to deliver his dialogue.

"Stop dreaming, start living. Don't be so melodramatic; be practical Vijay!" Sheela replied and signalled him to leave her bedroom first, through the toilet door, the way he had sneaked in a while ago.

Mumbai traffic was extremely slow because of the

festive season and weekend rush. So, Vijay reached back home fairly late. Vijay's parents, along with Vinita, had gone off to his maternal uncle's home in Satara, just for the festive weekend. Neeta was alone at home, fuming with anger. "Where were you all this while?" She demanded to know.

"I was in office, where else! The traffic was very slow that's why I got delayed. Anyway, why am I giving you an explanation? You won't believe it, come what may."

"I will believe only when you speak the truth. I called up on your office landline number in the afternoon. Your secretary told me that you left for home after lunch at 3 o'clock. And it's 9.30 now. It took you six and a half hours to reach back home! Did you come crawling?"

"How dare you call up the office to spy on me, you stupid woman!" Vijay was seething with hatred and anger now.

"Am I a stupid woman? I know exactly where you went. Let me check." She caught hold of his shirt, smelt it a couple of times and exclaimed, "You characterless man! Your shirt is smelling of the perfume that witch Sheela uses. So you made love with her, correct?"

"Why should I make love to her with my shirt on? You should smell my bare chest for confirmation. I'm sure you can easily recognise Sheela's body odour! You brainless, crazy woman! Go, kill yourself!" A badly cornered Vijay shouted back. Offence is the best way of defence.

Their bitter fighting continued endlessly. After about an hour, Neeta ran inside the bedroom and shut the door with a loud bang. Vijay was feeling very hungry, exhausted and disgusted. He gave a solid kick to the shut door and screamed, "Why don't you divorce me and go back to your parents in Nagpur? You will get the alimony you ask for and always in time, I can assure you."

"Oh yes! That's exactly what you want. But sorry, bad luck! You will never get a divorce from me. Let me see how you get married to that morally loose widow!"

In reply Vijay gave another kick to the door, a very hard one this time and shouted back, "You bloody idiot! Grow up! Or else, go kill yourself!"

It was nearing 12 o'clock. Feeling terribly hungry, Vijay went to the kitchen looking for some food. But he found nothing. It appeared that Neeta had not prepared dinner at all! He took out a small bottle of coke and four slices of brown bread from the fridge, applied peanut butter and jam liberally and ate quickly.

Realising that Neeta was not going to open the door for him to enter, he went to Vinita's bedroom and slept off, keeping the door open.

"Help! Help! Save me! Vijay, Vijay...."

Vijay jumped up from the bed and ran out. The screaming was coming from the kitchen. It was filled with smoke and smelling badly of burning flesh mixed with the foul smell of LPG! A human figure was on fire, running, jumping and screaming at the top of her voice! Oh my God! It was Neeta!

Vijay was shocked beyond belief but he had not lost his wits. He quickly pulled out the thick bedsheet from Vinita's bed and wrapped it around Neeta. She was very badly burnt by then. A mortally scared Neeta hugged him tightly and pleaded, "Vijay, save me! I don't want to die. Please save me...."

Before he could respond and act, the back portion of his shirt and front side of the trouser had caught fire. Vijay got panicky and tried to move away from Neeta but she wouldn't let go of him! It took a lot of brute force and nearly a minute to get rid of her deadly grip! As he freed himself, Neeta's body just bent backwards and fell. It was her last fall, with no more screams for help! Vijay ran to the nearest toilet to pour water over himself. He then took a bucketful of water and threw it over Neeta, dousing the fire instantly. But she had become still by then! Her body had become black, face unrecognisable! And he himself had received second degree burns!

He risked his life and somehow managed to close

the hot knob of the gas cylinder. The cylinder probably did not have much gas inside, so it didn't explode! The ambulance arrived after about ten minutes to take both of them to the burn injury centre. While waiting for the ambulance, Vijay called up his father, Neeta's parents and finally Sheela. All were shell-shocked to hear about what had happened. Though Vijay had realised that by now Neeta was no more, he decided not to tell anyone. He was sure by now that she had committed suicide by opening the LPG knob and setting herself on fire. He ran to their bedroom to check if she had left any suicide note. And it was there, on the dressing table, neatly kept under her mobile! He quickly picked it up and read, 'I am leaving this world! You are not worth living with. You are the worst husband one can have! I will not curse even my worst enemy to get a husband like you! I hate you!' There was no signature and no name. But the handwriting and the wording said it all! Vijay was sad because Neeta had died. But he felt very hurt reading her note. Was he really such a bad man? He tore the note and quickly burnt it.

Sheela was the first one to reach the hospital. By then Neeta was declared 'dead on arrival' and as per the medical norms, the police were informed immediately. Vijay told the police that most probably Neeta had gone to the kitchen to prepare something, as he had noticed a saucepan lying near the burners. The gas might have been left open accidentally by her in the evening. He had made sandwiches for himself in the dining area at midnight, so never went to the kitchen. But till proved otherwise, the police considered this as a case of either murder or suicide. So, he was, for the time being, officially arrested on charge of abetment to suicide. But he was allowed to remain hospitalised till he became fully fit, obviously guarded by the Mumbai police 24X7.

Vijay's parents and in-laws reached Mumbai in the evening. Neeta's body was handed over to the family after the post mortem. Unfortunately, Vijay was not in a state to attend her funeral. As it was an unfortunate accidental death, the Shradh was planned on the fourth day itself. In the intervening two days, Sheela managed to convince Neeta's distraught parents that her death was indeed an accident.

"Uncle and aunty, you knew your daughter extremely well, isn't it! Whatever she was, I'm sure she could not have committed suicide. Just for the sake of argument, if at all she wanted to, she could have used a sari or dupatta to hang herself from the ceiling fan! Why should she knowingly burn herself to death? Uncle no sane person would ever do that! And you know your son-in-law also too well. He is such a good man! Would he ever try to kill his own wife? And now, just think of it, if Vijay is kept in the lock-up on false charges, that too for a long time, then what will happen to his old parents? Moreover, who will look after Vinita, your only grandchild? She needs at least one parent now!"

Moved by Sheela's logical arguments, Neeta's parents finally told the police that they were fully convinced that their only daughter Neeta had died in an accidental fire and that they did not suspect any foul play. So, they didn't wish to press any charges against Vijay.

While recuperating on his hospital bed, Vijay kept on wondering about that unforgettable night. Why did Neeta set herself on fire? Why didn't she hang herself instead? And finally, why did she hug him so tightly? Was it because she was mortally scared to die? Or was she trying to get her husband also burnt to death? He couldn't find any answer to any of his questions.

After nearly ten days of treatment, Vijay was released from the hospital. At home he realised that Vinita was emotionally very disturbed. Even his own parents were not doing too well. The very next day, he took all of them to Shirdi on a two day trip. It was meant to get some relief from the sad and serious atmosphere at home. At Shirdi they all sincerely prayed for the well-being of the departed soul.

Vijay joined back office after returning from Shirdi. He had become a very serious, tough, and a no-nonsense manager! Under his strict command and control, Sheela's bakery business flourished further and reached new heights. She was extremely happy and felt thankful to him.

Since Neeta's death, Vijay had stopped sending any messages to Sheela, leave alone the shayaris. He would occasionally call her up only to discuss office matters in a serious tone and hang up immediately. She could very well understand his state of mind, so did not have any expectations either. Slowly the days became one full month, but Vijay did not start messaging. Sheela now started eagerly waiting for his 'Good Morning Sheela!' message, followed by his playful, romantic poems. She started missing him and secretly started longing for his company.

After nearly two months of waiting patiently, (or impatiently), Sheela decided to confront him. She called up the office landline number and requested him to visit her house in the afternoon the next day to discuss some urgent office matters. She waited the whole afternoon but he never came! Instead, his call came at around 5 pm.

"Sheela, I'm extremely sorry I could not come to your place."

"You could not come or you did not want to come to my place, Vijay! Please tell me the truth!"

"Can we discuss the urgent office matters on phone, Madam?" Vijay sounded very officious, avoiding any direct reply to her straightforward question.

"What is the matter with you, dear friend? Why do

you sound so very serious, so damn business-like these days? Don't we have a personal relationship? Now that you've indirectly but very clearly indicated that you don't want to meet me, can we talk a little about it please!"

"Past is past, let's forget it."

"No! How can we? Since the time Rushad died, you have been pestering me to rekindle our old love story. I rejected all your advances mainly because I did not wish to ruin your family and I didn't wish to complicate our lives. I had been controlling myself. And now…."

"And now what Sheela?" Vijay interjected.

"Now we both are single! You acted crazy about me till the other day! What has happened to you suddenly? Why don't you ask for my hand! Don't you love me anymore?"

"Sheela, please forgive me and forget about me. And, if you don't wish me to continue managing your business any longer, please tell me. I'll resign just now!"

"Why are you bringing office matters between us? You're doing an excellent job, you know it. Please tell me what the matter is! What is holding you back from coming back to me, to my life? Don't you wish to make love to me?" Sheela, unlike most other women, blurted out her sexual desire directly on phone! She desperately needed his company now, both emotionally and physically.

"I'm extremely sorry Sheela! I don't love you anymore.

Please forgive me. But, whenever you feel like, please come home to meet my parents and Vinita, your would-be daughter-in-law. That is, in case you really wish to make her one someday. I know she loves Rehan a lot. And I also think Rehan likes her too! Only you can ensure their childhood love blossoms into a flower one day! And that way we can remain related forever." He disconnected the call abruptly. He was crying uncontrollably now!

No one in this world except the doctor and the medical staff who had treated him would know that Vijay had suffered third degree burns in his groin area! He was rendered incapable of making love!

One Flight Stand

I started writing short stories almost a year ago. The plan was to write a total of nine stories and publish them as a book, but till now I've written only eight stories! The eighth one was completed almost a month back. Since then I've been scratching my head very hard for a suitable plot for the ninth one; but no luck so far! Fed up, I'm now contemplating publishing these eight stories only as a compilation. Let me think for another day or two before taking a final call. At times your brain goes really numb!

I have a bad (good!) habit of clearing all the junk mail from the mailbox once every fortnight, generally on a Monday. Maybe I like starting the week with a clean slate. Well, I really don't know. As everybody does, I was also going through the mails before deleting. Most of them were business oriented, with some stupid offers, as usual. But one particular mail caught my attention. It was not just another commercial solicitation but a private mail, a very small one at that. It read:

'Hi Groupie! I have been blessed with a baby boy just six days back. The saviour of the renowned 'Wahid dynasty of Karimnagar' has finally arrived! Thanks a lot for everything. Take care. Goodbye—Ayesha.'

Oh my God! I just couldn't believe my eyes. I read the mail thrice and then finally the truth dawned on me. Oh, yes! We have done it. I've finally made her a happy and proud mother. And I'm sure that she will definitely need my assistance at this crucial hour. It's my sacred duty to extend her all possible help. Even if she doesn't require any help, I must congratulate her straightaway. That's the least I must do now. So, I sent her a reply immediately.

She was not in my contact list earlier, and this is the very first mail from her since the time we met each other about ten months ago. Why has such an important mail from her been categorised as Junk? I really wish the system had some built-in system to differentiate between Junk and Important mail. Anyway, first I moved the mail to Inbox and then typed an emotional and congratulatory reply.

'Hello Ayesha! This is fantastic news! The much-awaited arrival of your baby has made me extremely proud and happy. Please accept my heartiest congratulations!

I'm sure both mother and son are doing fine. I'm in Delhi right now. Where are you at present—Hyderabad, Karimnagar or New Jersey? Please do let me know if I can be of any help to you. As already promised, the secret will remain with me till my very last breath. So, please don't worry. By the way, what have you named your son? I'm eager to know. Please reply ASAP.

Love and regards.

Groupie (your well wisher forever)

As I pressed the 'Send' button, the not-so-elaborate e-mail vanished from the monitor screen into the thin air, probably went to outer space, maybe hit the rough surface of the moon, the closest heavenly body, then finally recurved, and within no time knocked at Ayesha's inbox. Shortly after, a mail reached my inbox. Surprised by Ayesha's speedy reply, I immediately opened the mail to read it.

Alas! It was from the postmaster, a mail failure message! 'Unable to deliver to the mail address'.

Though I had sent the reply mail directly but I still cross-checked each letter of her mail id and 'Resend' my mail once again. But the same damn 'mail failure' message came for the second time. The email id was definitely used by Ayesha to send me the mail. Otherwise, I would not have received it at all. That meant only one of the two possible things—either Madam Ayesha had knowingly blocked me, probably immediately after dispatching her maiden mail, or, she had simply deleted her mail id. That meant Ayesha just didn't want me to contact her any longer! Maybe she was under stress, or the circumstances were too compelling!

I felt very sad. Such lovely news she has shared with me but I'm unable to convey my feelings back to her! Thinking about Ayesha, my mind went back to the day when we met each other for the first time, and the only time.

It was a cool April morning, 3.20 am to be precise. The 72 inch monitor hanging near Gate 26 of IGI Airport quietly and finally announced 'Boarding Now' for Air India 101, from Delhi to JFK International Airport, New York. No loud announcements are made here on the PA system; it's a silent airport after all. The flight was delayed by two hours. More than 90 per cent passengers are Indians on this flight. Soon nearly all of them got up and stood in a long queue, eager to board the aeroplane and fall asleep as soon as the flight took off. I sat facing the boarding gate, waiting for the crowd to thin down. After a good fifteen minutes, I got up and reached the gate straightaway. I was one of the last few to get inside the huge belly of Boeing 777. With a small sling bag containing my laptop, a book named *The*

Accidental Prime Minister and just one night's change, I gently pushed the still-unsettled crowd jostling around their respective seats and reached near mine—31A.

Whenever I travel long distances, I always go an extra mile to ensure I get a window seat. For that I take refuge in various ploys, on a case to case basis. These range from 'I've severe pain in my knee joints, so can't get up frequently to let others pass to and fro', to 'Hello beta, you look exactly like my younger daughter', to 'What a coincidence young man! You and my son (I don't have any) have the same name!' to a few other secret ones I can't reveal!

But 31A was occupied by an elderly lady, apparently in her late sixties! And a young, fairly beautiful, slender woman was occupying the aisle seat, probably her designated one. The centre one was obviously vacant. Standing very close, I looked down and smiled at the pretty woman; she smiled back. Then I looked further and gave a dirty look to her mother, the elderly one. She glanced at me briefly and then chose to look outside through the window, probably having a closer look at the rear part of the huge wing of this mighty aeroplane. Agitated, I cleared my throat loudly. She did turn her head this time. With hand gestures, I made her understand that she was occupying my seat. She gave a nervous smile and asked, "Can you take the centre seat?" I curtly shook my head rather vigorously. Maybe my speech-less approach made her think that I was deaf and dumb. Reluctantly she shifted her heavy, rounded Punjabi torso to the centre seat. I then collided with and brushed past a pair of jeans-clad knees, followed by a salwar-clad fat pair before finally settling down in 31A. Ah! Happiness at last!

Air India is probably the only airline in the entire world which employs cabin crew from a large spectrum—from handsome young boys to bald-headed potbellied men who are about to become senior citizens, and from eighteen-year-old virgins to 59 years 11 months 29 days old grandmothers! Well, I presume they don't take to the skies on the very last day, the day of retirement! When the door closed, the elderly airhostess announced that Air India 101 would reach Vienna after an eight and a half hours long flight, have two hours refuelling halt there and then get airborne for a further ten-hour flight all the way to our final destination, New York. There was a near pin drop silence inside the aircraft! Probably all passengers were quietly praying, 'God save us from this terrible long torture!'

Air India 101 actually makes a non-stop long haul of 15 hours to reach JFK directly. But thanks to our enemy-till-eternity neighbour Pakistan, all civil flights are now prohibited to fly over Pakistan airspace, thereby forcing majority of airliners to take a long detour to reach Europe and USA.

I spent the first leg sleeping, eating, sleeping again and watching a stupid Hollywood movie in between. As my initial interaction with my immediate neighbour was not a sweet one, and also she looked like one of those 'Subhash Nagar' type Dilli-wali behenjis, I avoided speaking to her. So, overall, it was a boring journey. Maybe she too got bored sitting next to me. So, after an unscheduled and gruelling four-hour-long refuelling halt at Vienna, when departure was finally announced, she shifted to the aisle seat. The daughter now sat next to me. With enough rest in the last leg, both my body and soul were feeling quite fresh. With the young woman shifting to the centre seat, my mind also felt recharged!

Writers are always looking for stories everywhere. So, they never waste opportunities to speak to people, known or unknown. I had held myself back from speaking with the earlier neighbour but now it was high time.

The pretty woman didn't appear to be another behenji. A behenji's daughter need not necessarily be another behenji! So, I straightaway started in English. "So, you have finally decided to give some relief to your mother!"

"You are grossly mistaken Mister. She is not my mother; I don't even know her. She is just a co-passenger," retorted the pretty woman.

"What! Oh God, I'm so sorry. But then why have

you changed your seat? Why unnecessarily make yourself uncomfortable for next ten-twelve hours, that too for the sake of someone you don't even know properly?" I asked.

"Actually, she pleaded with me for a change of seat saying that she has problem of frequent urination. I simply obliged her."

"Well, I don't think that's true. During the previous flight from Delhi to this place, she hardly went to the toilet, maybe just once or twice, isn't it! Sorry to say this, but I think she has managed to fool you," I stated simply.

"Yes, I am aware of everything. But she is an old lady, a senior citizen. I think I can do this much for her. So, I came here to sit next to you," she smilingly said.

"Oh! That's so very kind of you! By the way, I'm eagerly looking for someone to speak with; it has been so damn boring so far!" I instantly extended my hand towards her.

She shook my hand and said, "Hi! I am Ayesha, Ayesha Wahid from New Jersey, a so-called NRI."

I quickly introduced myself. Her eyes brightened up the moment I told her about my Air Force background. "What a coincidence! My dad was a Brigadier in the Army. Brig Shamshad, now retired, of course. By any chance, do you know him?"

"Sorry Ayesha, I have never met him. India is such a big country; I distinctly remember I met one of my flying training course mates after about sixteen years, as a senior Wing Commander! But I'm extremely happy to meet you, the beautiful, young daughter of another fauji officer."

"Oh, never mind that, everyone doesn't know everybody in this world!" She sounded a bit philosophical.

"Well said young lady. You know very well that as per our unwritten but strictly followed defence services norms, wards of an officer will, by default, address other officers as uncle. I'm a retired Group Captain and fifty-one now. So, by this norm, you should call me uncle. But personally, I really don't mind you addressing me as 'Groupie'. Or for that matter, you may even call me by my name. I have a nice, catchy name after all!" I said in a joking but at the same time, matter-of-fact manner.

"I'm thirty-six now and heavily married, married off at twenty-two. So, it's just a fifteen year age gap. And you are indeed a very handsome man. Secondly, right now we are both out of the defence services and more importantly, out of the country. So, for me, 'Uncle' is out. It is too downmarket! But at the same time, I won't like to address you by your first name, that too at our very first meeting. That's against our custom, tradition and culture. So, 'Groupie' is just fine with me. And now that we have introduced ourselves to each other, I definitely wish to know more about you." She was embarrassingly straightforward! I felt highly elated too—a fifty-one years old handsome man! That too coming from a beautiful young woman! Oh God!

I instinctively clasped her right hand with both mine and confessed, "Thank you so very much for calling me a handsome man. I really don't know whether you actually mean it or are just pulling my leg! But I do admire your frankness, as expected from the daughter of an officer! Now please allow me also to be frank with you. I really don't know how you managed to pass your time but I was thoroughly bored in the last twelve hours or so. Let's make up for all that now, shall we?"

"Same here. Let's start with you. What I know is that our defence officers retire as per their last rank and the minimum retirement age is fifty-two. Correct? Then how come you call yourself a Retired Group Captain of Indian Air Force at 51? How's that possible?" She questioned.

With keen and mutual interest, we both now turned inwards and sat comfortably facing each other. We forgot that we had started talking to each other just a couple of minutes ago.

"I'm thoroughly impressed with your common sense and intelligence, Ayesha! You are absolutely right. Actually, for a Flying Branch Officer of my rank in the Air Force, the superannuation age is fifty-four but because of some pressing family issues, I had opted for premature retirement at fifty, which is known as PR. I now live on pension and some savings. I'm also trying my hand and luck as a writer. I'm an Aquarius born in the latter part of January, 28th to be exact. By any chance, are you a Sagittarian?" I was very interested to know and I had a valid reason for that.

"To be extremely honest about it, my community in general, and I myself in particular don't believe in astrology much. But what a coincidence once again! My date of birth is 28 November so I am a Sagittarian? But why did you ask that?"

My face brightened up. "Oh my God! I may sound a bit downmarket, but I somehow believe in Astrology, Sixth Sense and Telepathy. I just had a gut feeling that you would turn out to be a Sagittarian. And here you are! You know what, some astrologers say that though they are temperamentally different, Aquarians and Sagittarians get naturally attracted to each other, just like the opposite poles of a magnet! Also, believe me Ayesha, telepathy plays a big role in majority of people's lives. It has happened with me so many times, at so many places, on so many occasions. Just think hard—have you ever thought of or remembered someone on a particular day and met that very person, absolutely unexpectedly, out of turn, the very next moment or the same day?" I ended with a question.

"Though I have never believed in these things but I do have a little knowledge about them. I never tried to find out the influences of the stars and numerology in my life seriously. But wait a minute! As far as telepathy goes, I think it has happened with me once. While in college, one day I was badly missing and remembering an old classmate of mine from the school days. After some hours she appeared from nowhere, that very evening! We both had a gala time together. However, I don't really know if it was telepathy or just a coincidence!" She admitted candidly.

Heading westwards, our aeroplane had levelled out at 34,000 feet. The cabin crew started pushing the trolley around offering drinks, for the first time since we got airborne from Delhi. When the ever-smiling (plastic smile I safely assumed) airhostess looked at both of us, I politely asked for beer, my all-time favourite. She gave me a can of beer and a miniature pouch of snacks, monkey nuts to be precise! Ayesha asked for red wine and received a small bottle and a small pouch of monkey nuts, what else! Our elderly neighbour settled for a fruit juice. As the airhostess started pushing the trolley to serve the row behind us, I enquired, "Excuse me, Miss! Would you be coming back for a second round?"

"I'm sorry sir, but no repeat of drinks," she declared.

"Well, in that case, can you give both of us one more please! It's a very long flight, you see. And you never served us anything in the last flight, though it was eight hours long!" I fought my case fairly diligently.

The otherwise seasoned airhostess felt apologetic and quickly handed over another can of beer and a bottle of red wine to me and Ayesha. I looked up and smilingly said "snacks?"

The airhostess grinned and handed over two more packets of monkey nuts.

Ayesha and I said 'Cheers' with the can and the glass bottle softly colliding with each other and opened our snack packets to munch. In the midst of a prolonged journey to a faraway land, after two long sips of beer had gone down my throat, I felt quite relaxed. Ayesha also seemed to be in a happy state of mind. After a brief period of silence, while still munching peanuts, we restarted our friendly chat.

"You know what Ayesha, all my life, I've always wondered about this monkey nut thing, as to why it is called so? It neither resembles the shape nor the size of a monkey's head! On the other hand, a walnut actually resembles a human brain. So, it should have been called Man-nut. And though I never had the privilege or misfortune of eating a monkey's head in my entire life, I don't think that it will actually taste like these monkey nuts!" I seriously stated.

"Ha...ha... related to this enthralling topic of

discussion, do you have some really interesting story in your kitty. Please go ahead, enlighten me! Let's get entertained!" Ayesha urged.

I gave her an admiring look and smiled; she smiled back. That encouraged me to tell her a story, a decade old story. "By the way, talking about monkey nuts, a European friend of mine had once visited a very popular local bar in the capital city of one of the far eastern countries. Sorry, I won't name the country. Anyways, the bar had different sections and was extremely crowded. In one section he saw a live Cobra, tied up above one of the bar counters with its tail hanging loose, with a small cut at the end. My friend went closer to watch what actually happens. He saw the barman pouring different but all neat drinks in glasses, as demanded by the customers. He held each glass just below the Cobra-tail for a few seconds before serving it to the customer. On closer inspection, my friend saw the barman was squeezing the Cobra-tail to ensure that just a few drops and not more of blood fell into the glass from its cut! People were freaking out. It is considered quite healthy there! Though feeling very edgy about it, he doled out some extra money and had a peg of neat scotch with drops of Cobra blood in it. Well, it tasted a bit weird but nothing happened! In another section he noticed people savouring fried cockroaches as snacks. He later visited the most secluded, premium, circular enclosure, by dishing out a small fortune at the guarded entrance! He was thoroughly searched for any cameras and was asked to deposit his smartphone at the baggage counter.

A little ahead, at the centre of the enclosure, a small monkey was kept in a seated position, tied up to the central pole. The poor monkey's scull was cut open and its brain was visible to the public gathered around. Probably the monkey was heavily sedated as it sat motionless, eerily quiet! Surprisingly, everyone in the small crowd was drinking whisky and each one was holding a steel spoon with a rather longish handle! My wealthy, inquisitive friend was also handed such a spoon and a glass of whisky on arrival. Unable to understand the usage of the spoon, he looked at the crowd for a clue. But there was none! After about five-seven minutes of waiting, a burly figure appeared from behind the curtain with a small bucket of steaming hot oil with a ladle inside it. The crowd suddenly went ecstatic! They all started making awful noises. The burly man went near the monkey, and to my friend's horror, he took out the ladle and using that started pouring boiling oil from the small bucket over the monkey's split open brain! The poor animal shook a bit but did not give out any shrill cry! Its small brain started boiling and the frenzied crowd immediately started scooping it up by using their long spoons. They started eating the monkey's semi-cooked brain as a snack!! My poor friend threw the spoon and ran towards the toilet to puke! He was lying sick in his hotel room for almost three days afterwards."

"Yuck! How horrible! But that's just a story, not a true one, isn't it?" Ayesha sounded very confident.

"It's a true story," I quickly replied with a wicked smile on my face. She looked confused.

"Can we change the topic, please? It sounds so awful!"

"Okay, point taken. Let's talk of something else. You are a smart, educated, young, beautiful daughter of an army officer. So what did you exactly mean when you said, 'I was married off at twenty-two'? Were you forced?" I fired a straight question.

Ayesha took a long sip to finish off her first bottle of wine and put the empty bottle in the net provided at the back of the seat in front of her. She now slowly folded her legs and sat comfortably to face me directly.

"As you said earlier, and I admit it, I have been an intelligent student from childhood. After completing B Tech with flying colours, I too chased the 'Great American Dream' and got a job offer from USA, a company in New Jersey to be precise. Both my parents belong to Hyderabadi Muslim families. Dad is indeed very progressive. Though my Mom is a housewife, but after spending some part of her married life in army cantonments she has become semi-liberal. Unfortunately, most of our close relatives are quite orthodox and backward. They just would not allow me to go to the USA all alone. And to top it all, they soon managed to convince my mother to join their incorrigible gang too. Thereafter, all my coaxing, pleading and emotional blackmailing fell on deaf ears. On the other hand, I was very adamant that come what may, I would go to USA! No force on this earth could stop me! My intelligent, dear dad finally brokered peace with a unique formula of his—to get me married to an NRI before leaving India. Delighted, all our crazy relatives frantically started searching for a suitable boy—Hyderabadi by birth, Muslim by religion, Engineer by education, Software Developer by profession and finally, New Jersey by location. After an all-out global search, within a month's time, they finally found one such man. He matched all the requirements except one. He was not a Hyderabadi by birth, but belonged to a small village near Karimnagar in Andhra Pradesh itself. So, with just about two weeks left to fly out to the USA, I was hurriedly married off to Nadeem Wahid, an NRI, my present and only husband. I was just twenty-two then!" Ayesha sounded a bit nostalgic, maybe sad too.

"Oh, I'm so sorry to know that. But at the end of the day, you are happily married, isn't it?" I asked.

"I think I had said that I'm Heavily Married." She

heaved a sigh and deliberately looked the other way. I found myself dumbfounded. I sensed things were not all right between the husband and wife.

"Anyways! Enough about me. You had started the conversation by saying you are a writer. How do you pick up a story? And once you finalise a storyline, how do you build up on it? I mean the place, time, characters, the conversations and the ending—I mean the climax etc." Ayesha resumed the conversation after a pause. She wanted to know it all at one go.

"You know dear, the lawyers make a mountain out of a molehill. But we, the writers make mountains; I mean a number of those, out of a single molehill! You have to build a web of words, sentences and dialogues around your selected plot and characters in order to make them look real and acceptable to the public. Take today's case. This unexpected meeting of ours in-flight, that too because you were coaxed to change your seat by the Dilli-wali behenji sitting next to you, may turn out to be a fantastic, beautifully written, well-acclaimed story! And a few years later, some renowned director might just decide to make a movie out of it too, you never know!" I sounded very optimistic and thoroughly professional!

"Impressed, truly impressed I am Groupie! I'm convinced and very sure by now that you are indeed a damn good novelist. So, how many books have you written and published by now? Must be quite a few…"

"Thanks for the compliment friend though I don't think I actually deserve it. But I must tell you one thing; like Hollywood and Bollywood, ours is also a big, bad world. You might have heard the story of Chetan Bhagat, India's number one novelist at present. He went to scores of publishers with his novels but everyone rejected him. He struggled for a long time, and really struggled very hard. Finally, after many years, one fine day he succeeded. And now, those same publishers queue up outside his house!" I sounded as if I was making a case for myself.

"Yeah, of course I know about Chetan Bhagat, in fact, I'm a big fan of his writing. Whenever I visit India, I always pick up his latest novel. But why did you mention him?"

I quickly polished off my first can of beer and continued, "Ayesha, what I'm trying to tell you is that this newfound friend of yours is still a struggler in the writers world. I first tried to publish a compilation of poems titled *Hello India,* but all publishing houses turned me down saying that they just don't publish poems these days as there are no buyers. So, finally I e-published them in a popular online bookstore. Probably those publishers were right because hardly a few were sold! Later, I wrote a fairly decent novel, well, that's what I myself felt about it. I also gave the novel a nice, modern, catchy name, *Luv. Com.* Once again I was refused by all publishers quoting various silly reasons. Disgusted, I put that also in the e-bookstore. But not too many sales, this time too! So, after a while, can you believe what I did?"

"Please don't play puzzle-dazzle! What did you do? Spent your own money to self-publish it?" Ayesha was curious.

"You guessed that wrong! Do you wish to avail one more chance? Maybe you wish to go for 'Best of Three' options, beautiful young lady!" I teased her.

"Thanks a ton for your generous offer but I'm not going for it, handsome old man! Please carry on with your narrative." We had started with our second round of drinks by then, both feeling very relaxed and high-spirited.

"Well, during that time, a small news item was published in the newspapers that the original author of *Mast Ram* series had died. I don't remember his real name. Have you heard anything about his writings?" I asked her and immediately realised what a stupid thing I'd done! I think I've crossed the 'Laxman-Rekha'; I'm sure this time I've embarrassed her badly, I thought.

Ayesha smiled mischievously and spoke up, "In my engineering college days I read one of his books. It was very thin and by no standards a proper novel. He wrote erotica, correct?"

It was my turn to feel embarrassed. I looked at her and smiled nervously.

"Hai Allah! Look at you! Your cheeks have gone red!

Don't feel so embarrassed Groupie! We both are 'heavily married', aren't we? And as youngsters, girls also enjoy their lives, have fun! Except having sex, I did everything else, including drugs, though only once. Most girls do!" Ayesha put me at ease, instantly.

"I'm sorry but am feeling fine now. You are a fantastic woman, Ayesha. I really envy your husband, lucky man!" I paused a little for the impact but she looked serious; maybe the last sentence was uncalled for. Unabated, I continued, "As I mentioned, with the news of the death of the author of *Mast Ram* series, an idea clicked in my brain. I just withdrew my novel from the e-bookstore temporarily, quickly changed the title to *Mast Ram Alive* and relaunched it the very next day. And you know what, the sales picked up slowly and steadily."

"What! Don't tell me you did that! You've actually changed your book's name to *Mast Ram Alive*? Seriously?" Ayesha could not believe me.

"Really, Ayesha! I'm not joking with you. You can always crosscheck in an e-bookstore," I assured her.

"Yes, you are right; I can always verify that after reaching New Jersey. I do have a Kindle but, unfortunately, I kept it in my checked-in baggage. But seriously, I'm amazed to know that a mere change of a title has done the trick! Okay, what's next! Have you written any other book?"

"Currently I'm working on a number of short stories. I've already finished writing three stories and am planning to write six more, to make a compilation of nine short stories. So I'm looking for, or you could say frantically searching for ideas. Do you have any interesting or gripping life-story to share?" I eagerly asked.

"Not really. I've lived a plain and simple life so far. No complications, so no stories. And, by the way, how do you write the stories? I mean in a big, fat notebook, finally making a huge manuscript out of it or something similar?" Ayesha wanted to know.

"Ha...ha...ha… nothing of that sort. In today's IT world everyone resorts to typing. All stories, poems and novels are typed on the laptop. Some great novelists (I mean the rich ones) even hire professionals who hear them narrating a story and convert that to a written one! I am a poor man, you see! So, I type it out on the laptop, all by myself."

"But why only nine stories? Why not ten?"

"Good question young lady! Nine Planets, Emperor Akbar's 'Navratna' (Nine Gems), Nine pins, Nine holes, and Cat O' Nine tails! Got it?"

"Ok, understood. By any chance have you already named this collection of short stories?" She appeared keen to know more about my writing.

"Yes, I've called it The Bangkok Fiasco and Other

Stories. I revealed the name of my forthcoming release and genuinely wanted to check her immediate reaction.

"It's a good name. But why such a name?"

"If you look at yourself and all the human beings around, you will realise that human life is basically an assortment of short stories. Some stories are romantic ones, a few tragic, some sceptic, and a few opportunistic. There are stories of hope, of despair, of utmost care, of utter negligence, of vengeance, of values and also of disrespect. So, in this book of mine, I'm basically trying to show how we Indians behave in different situations, and with different people. That's why I chose such a name," I replied, rather explained myself.

"Oh! That's really nicely explained. A nice title, indeed." She sounded excited.

"Thanks for your compliment. But believe me, Ayesha, if this title does not work out well, like the last time, I will change this name too! Maybe I will rename it as *Mast Ram Short Ones* or *Short Shots of Mast Ram* or simply *Mast Ram Quickies*! It might work again!" I think I spoke with negativity and a little desperation.

"Groupie, please don't be so negative; things will work out fine, trust me. Now please tell me one thing, are you carrying your laptop? And if so, can I read one of your stories if you don't mind? I'm really quite interested to see how a novelist writes!" Ayesha appeared very keen.

"Yes friend, I'm carrying my laptop and all the stories are written and stored in it. I'll bring it down from the overhead cabin soon, only for you. But please don't mind, I'll allow you to read just one. And that will happen only after lunch because now I can smell chicken curry and steaming basmati rice. I have a very strong sense of smell, you see. Lunch is being served, so let's do bottoms up!" I held my second beer can up. Ayesha also raised her wine bottle to the same level, for one last cheering. We both finished off our drinks and eagerly waited for the service trolley, with a smiling airhostess behind it, to appear.

We ate our food quietly. Both had non-veg lunch, and it was hot and tasty. After everything was cleared up by the cabin crew, all three of us visited the washroom turn by turn, I being the last one. I took out the laptop from the overhead baggage-hold before settling down in my seat. The elderly woman in 31C continued to ignore me. To hell with her!

Like a good ex-fauji, I had charged the laptop before boarding the flight. So, I just switched it on, opened the first page of the story titled '21.12.2112' and handed it to Ayesha to read. She read the very first sentence and quickly looked at me, appearing a little shocked. I was expecting it; so I just smiled and signalled her to continue reading. She went back to the story. As the title suggests, it is a story dated almost one hundred years into the future.

Basically, it's a kind of science fiction where a number of probable happenings are chronologically listed. I was watching Ayesha closely. Her expressions kept changing as she continued to read through it.

"Wow! This is really a superb story! Very informative, engrossing and at the same time very interesting." Her twinkling eyes gave me an appreciative look while doling out the verdict.

"Ayesha, Ayesha! Please don't praise my creativity so much! I don't think it's so damn good," I pleaded with her, though I was feeling elated at her comments. She was the first person, other than me obviously, to read the story.

"No Groupie, I really mean it. If your other stories are also equally interesting, then no one can stop you from becoming a famous author, believe me!"

"Thanks a lot, dear! Now please tell me which part of it you liked the most," I enquired.

She gave me a mischievous smile once again, turned back the pages and pointed to the news report dated 2025 AD. It read:

2025 AD–Here comes the funniest and at the same time the most useful news item of this century. As per the epic *Mahabharata*, Draupadi was specially blessed by God to regain her virginity after every sexual encounter so that she could satisfy each one of her five legally married husbands. Taking a cue and inspiration from this story, an

Indian scientist couple settled in the USA has managed to develop a Combo, a tonic for sipping and a special Gel for internal use by women. These ensure that a woman continues to remain a virgin, well, nearly one! The Tamil scientist named Shri Mahalingam and his equally bright wife have taken pains to find a suitable name for their unique product 'Vagino-Moto'. This has changed the entire outlook towards sex, worldwide! Men and women are so happy now. Fresh feeling each night, every time! The sales graph of this product has bypassed all expectations.

Oh my God! Out of so many interesting ones, she picked this one only? I think I got the hint! So, I quickly took back my laptop, closed it deftly, put it aside and looked straight into her eyes to ask, "If you really had a choice, would you have actually used it?"

"Yes, of course? As you've mentioned in it, 'fresh feeling every time', so, why not?" She shot back. She, too, kept staring at me. I was amazed at her honesty and boldness.

Honestly, I did not have the moral courage, I mean 'guts' in simpler terms, to discuss nuances of sex organs of the fairer sex with her. It is not proper, I thought to myself. But still, I couldn't disregard and discard her hint just like that, if at all there was one. So, I now decided to ask her a direct question. "Ayesha, how many children do you have? All were normal deliveries or caesareans?"

She quickly glanced at the passenger occupying 31C. She was fast asleep after a heavy lunch. Ayesha gave me a pensive look, clasped my right hand and replied, "Groupie, I am childless! A barren woman!" Her eyes became moist and tears started rolling down her cheeks.

I was caught absolutely off-guard. She was crying continuously, silently, with her head down. I, with my free hand, gently held her chin up and made her look at me. I whispered, "I'm extremely sorry, Ayesha. Please forgive me for asking! But, please tell me, what do the doctors say? Is there something wrong with you? I'm sure they can fix it."

"Please don't feel sorry about it. Fortunately, there is nothing wrong with me. I have been taken to at least a dozen doctors in India by my in-laws and also to quite a few in the USA by Nadeem himself. All my systems have been certified as fully functional, over and over again! Otherwise, sorry to say this, but by now my in-laws would have ensured Triple-Talaq for me and a second nikah for my husband," Ayesha replied slowly, in between sobs.

"Ok! Got it! There is some problem with your hubby then," I surmised.

"Not exactly a problem. You can call it a peculiar medical condition, that too a self-created one, an unbelievable one at that." This time she spoke with some composure.

"Ayesha, I don't quite get this. What is that 'self-created medical condition'? And why do you call it unbelievable?" I was genuinely perplexed.

"You had told me before lunch that your first novel was not selling at all till you renamed it. Isn't that an unbelievable story? Similarly, I'm unable to get impregnated by my husband because he has extremely low sperm count! And what's more this is because of quite an extraordinary, unbelievable reason!" She said.

"And what on earth is that?" I straightaway asked her.

"That's because being a villager by birth, Nadeem, since his teenage days, has been wearing that typical chequered, mostly green colour lungi of his, with an extremely tight knot around his lower waist! And that has done the trick!" Ayesha blurted out the startling information.

"What? What crap, what nonsense are you saying? How can that be? I don't believe you, Ayesha! At least, not this one! No way!"

"I just knew it, Groupie! You men are all the same, across the world! You say things which are quite abstract, and we, the womenfolk believe you. But when we tell you something, that too something as exactly told by a doctor, you don't believe it. And, that's just because you have never heard of such a thing before! This is not done!" She was half-hurt, half-angry by now.

"Sorry, sorry! I'm extremely sorry to doubt you, Ayesha. But it sounds so damn funny and untrue!" Sensing her foul mood, I immediately held her hands and apologised.

"I'm a B Tech and an MBA. If I say something you better believe me! But like you, my well-educated husband also never believed me and the doctors. He always wears a lungi and a sando banian at home. And at that, he continues to tie his God-damned lungi so very tightly! Which NRI wears a lungi at home? That too while living in USA? Crazy man!" Ayesha started crying inconsolably.

Ayesha was still holding my right hand with hers. I instinctively pulled her towards me. Using her free left hand, she quickly pushed the handrest between our seats behind and hugged my chest! She continued sobbing while hugging me tightly. My hands slowly moved around her slim waist, tightening our hug. Her face almost touched mine.

After a heavy lunch, almost everyone was dozing off. So, no one noticed our closeness.

In between spurts of sobs, Ayesha started whispering near my ear, "You know Groupie, I belong to a fauji family, decently educated, widely travelled and above all, broad minded. But unfortunately, my husband is from a rural background. His family never checked him, never

ever corrected him. Instead, though fully aware of the actual cause of our problem, they always chose to blame me just because I'm a woman!"

"But what about your husband? He doesn't tell them anything? Doesn't he ask them to shut up?" I whispered my question into her ears.

"Nadeem is otherwise a reasonably good-natured person. But, for reasons not understood by me so far, he never ever speaks or does anything against any of his family members. So much so, he always negates the advice given by all the doctors in India and abroad by saying that his own father also wears a lungi very tightly, but still he was born to him. What can you say to that? Aberrations are everywhere, in all walks of life, isn't it! But how can you change such a man's line of thinking? Tell me!" Her thin pink lips almost touched my earlobe.

"I now understand how difficult your life is! But tell me one thing Ayesha, why haven't you adopted one or two children by now? What is holding you back?" My lips touched her earlobe as I asked. It was a soft touch but a deliberate move from my side and she did not move back even an inch! It was the best in-flight feeling I ever had!

"Sheer hope! Yes, sheer hope that one fine day I will conceive. But a number of doctors have already warned me that with Nadeem's present abysmally low sperm count, I will never get pregnant. Secondly, his family seriously thinks that only our own son, own heir can carry forward the legacy of the clan. What clan? And what legacy? As if theirs is not a middle-class family but a historical dynasty, like Emperor Akbar's or Emperor Ashoka's. So, it's a strict No for adoption!" She quipped but in a very hushed tone.

"Oh, I see. This is really a very peculiar situation. I think now I understand your words 'heavily married'. You are indeed heavily married and not happily married. I'm rather lucky that way, I must confess." I sympathised with her.

"You know what hurts me the most Groupie? As long as I'm in USA, working and with no relatives hovering around at our residence, there is not much of a problem. But the moment someone from his family visits us or I step into India, especially to his small village near Karimnagar, people start calling me *Baanjh* (sterile)! It really hurts! In a male dominated society like ours, women get blamed for everything! I feel so helpless, so damn disgusted!" As Ayesha spoke, her hug tightened further, probably looking for comfort.

"Yeah, you are right Ayesha. That terrible Indian word *Baanjh* really hits a woman hard, very hard! And especially when you are not at fault. Surprisingly, there is no such matching word for unfertile males! So unfortunate!"

Before speaking further, Ayesha put her head up and

glanced around. No one was looking at us. Cuddling couples are a common sight on board long international flights. Ayesha suddenly put her hands around my neck. She brought her mouth extremely close to my ear and whispered, "You know my biological clock is ticking very fast. So, Groupie, can you please give me a baby? Don't say no, please! I beg of you!"

I just could not believe my ears! She had whispered into my right ear only, with her lips securely placed over and moving within the geographical limits of the earlobe. The other ear possibly tried to eavesdrop very hard but could hear nothing! It was a terrific physical feeling! And it took me a few seconds to actually fathom her request. I was literally shell-shocked!

"Do you mean that I become a sperm donor for you? And you get artificially inseminated by that in a registered fertility clinic?"

Ayesha laughed. It was a sad laugh, more of a chuckle, with a mixed feeling of humiliation, helplessness, pain, suffering and amusement. "Those who are not willing to adopt a child, even from very close relatives, will accept sperm from any Tom, Dick or Harry! Have you gone crazy?"

"Then how, Ayesha?" I asked simply.

"Groupie, I have always been faithful to my husband. But I've also been subjected to terrible verbal abuse for a very long time. Over the years, it has become so unbearable that now I am left with only two options—either cheat him once to have a baby outside the marriage thereby making the family happy forever or just leave this world by committing suicide! I mean it, Groupie, I really mean it! I'm financially rich but emotionally a pauper!" She sounded very determined about her course of action. I got worried.

"Ayesha, please don't ever think of committing suicide. Each one of us has got just one human life, so we must live it fully. And honestly speaking, a one-time-act to make yourself, your family and the entire clan happy forever shouldn't be termed as 'cheating'. It is rather a perfect demonstration of your devotion, love and commitment towards your husband and his family. Okay dear, I'll definitely help you. Now please tell me what exactly do you want me to do? But before that, please clarify one thing, why me?"

"Well, like my Dad, you are also a defence officer. Absolutely nothing against civilians, but to become a service officer you have gone through the tough selection process of the Services Selection Boards. That means you have been certified to possess very high level of IQ, physical fitness and good common sense. And other officer-like qualities of honesty, integrity, truthfulness have come to you quite naturally, especially after serving in defence for such a long time. Also, after interacting with you for the last few hours, I've realised that you are a good man with special artistic inclination. And I really want my kid to imbibe all these qualities. I'm basically an introvert by nature yet, I just felt like chatting with you the moment I sat next to you. And now, I don't really understand how I'm saying all these things to you, but I've already, though indirectly, hinted to you that I wish to have physical intimacy with you! Allah! Please forgive me!" Ayesha looked up towards the aeroplane roof.

"Thanks for praising me so much though I don't deserve most of it. But let me make one thing very clear, Ayesha! I'm fully aware that it's an irresistible offer. But it won't be possible for me to stay in your house or somewhere close by in New Jersey for a while. I'm going to remain very busy while in USA," I pointed out. I really had a tight schedule ahead.

"Oh, I forgot to tell you, I had gone to my husband's ancestral house in Karimnagar for two weeks as my mother-in-law was terribly sick. During that period, Nadeem's paternal aunt came to New Jersey for a month-long visit, basically to cook for him. So, she will be with us for two more weeks," she announced.

"Then what? And how?" My simple question.

In reply, her mouth touched my ear once again and murmured something which sent shock waves through my spine!

"Let's do it here, in-flight!"

"Oh, no! No way! Have you gone nuts, Ayesha," I exclaimed.

"Sorry! But we don't have any other option left. You suggest one," she quickly replied.

I was feeling terribly excited and horribly scared at the same time. There were butterflies flying around inside my stomach and my heart was doing a wild dance! Still a bright idea suddenly came to my mind. I exclaimed, "Hey! Just wait a minute! Some days back I had seen a video clipping in WhatsApp. A couple feels horny in-flight; they plan things quietly and after a while suddenly start fighting with each other very loudly. The passengers feel very disturbed, so they head for the nearest toilet and lock themselves up. They do whatever they wanted to do inside, all the while screaming at each other."

"So! You want us to scream at each other? Make a scene here? Not done!"

"No, of course not. I have a better idea," and I whispered the idea directly into her ear. She nodded in excitement and gave me a tight hug.

After about two minutes, as per our plan, Ayesha left her seat, jumped over the sleeping co-passenger and ran towards the toilet, covering her mouth with both hands as if trying to control vomiting. Almost immediately, I too picked up a bottle of mineral water and ran behind her, straight inside the toilet, trying to help her out!

And I latched the door behind quickly. We opened the toilet door after about ten minutes and found an eager airhostess waiting outside. "What happened? Hope everything is alright?" She enquired.

"Oh, yes. She had a sudden bout of nausea. It's okay now, thanks," I replied straightaway. Ayesha was looking down, with a pink hanky covering her mouth.

"Which seat numbers are you two occupying? I will get some puke bags and medicine for you soon."

"31A and B. Thanks a lot." I thanked the visibly concerned airhostess and tugged at Ayesha to follow me slowly towards our seats.

I wrapped a shawl around both of us and sat quietly. After everything was over, it was a time for introspection. I had lectured Ayesha a while ago but now I felt that I had cheated on my wife! I should not have listened to Ayesha! It's all her fault! But is it, really? A man starts repenting only after the act, never before! And always blames the other party.

Ayesha put her head on my chest and cried silently, wetting my shirt. I could not understand the reason. Was it joy? Or was it sadness? Or repentance? Or just another nice, feminine way of thanking me! I decided not to ask her. We never spoke with each other.

A few hours later, at the luggage belt in JFK Airport we collected our bags. She looked at me and spoke up, "Thank you, Groupie."

"Thank you, Ayesha. Wish you all the very best. We will meet again, God willing. Take care." I replied pensively.

"Inshallah!" she echoed. We hugged each other briefly one last time and parted.

...Finally, I have got my ninth and the last story. Didn't I predict this just ten months back? Thank you so very much, Ayesha! For the story and also for everything else! You're really a darling.

But what do I name this story? 'Love in the Air' or 'Love in the Flight'? No, not gelling! How about 'One Night Stand'? Nice popular name, but frankly speaking, we never spent the night together! Oh, wait! Something bright is tickling my brain! Okay, I got it now! 'One Flight Stand'. Yes, that's it! Great name indeed, isn't it?

Note: This is an imaginary story, 100 per cent, I swear! I am a heavily married man, after all!